NUNCLE

NEIL J COOK

The Book Guild Ltd

First published in Great Britain in 2024 by
The Book Guild Ltd
Unit E2 Airfield Business Park,
Harrison Road, Market Harborough,
Leicestershire. LE16 7UL
Tel: 0116 2792299
www.bookguild.co.uk
Email: info@bookguild.co.uk
X : @bookguild

Copyright © 2024 Neil J Cook

The right of Neil J Cook to be identified as the author of this
work has been asserted by them in accordance with the
Copyright, Design and Patents Act 1988.

All rights reserved. No part of this publication may be
reproduced, transmitted, or stored in a retrieval system, in any form or by any means,
without permission in writing from the publisher, nor be otherwise circulated in
any form of binding or cover other than that in which it is published and without
a similar condition being imposed on the subsequent purchaser.

This work is entirely fictitious and bears no resemblance to any persons living or dead.

Typeset in 10.5pt Adobe Garamond Pro

Printed on FSC accredited paper
Printed and bound in Great Britain by 4edge Limited

ISBN 978 1835740 200

British Library Cataloguing in Publication Data.
A catalogue record for this book is available from the British Library.

For my children

PROLOGUE

Date: XXXXXXX
Urgent Memo
From the desk of: REDACTED

To: XXXXXX
...to continue, with the biosphere collapsing, the continued survival of the human species is under threat. This collapse is accelerating social, economic and ecological issues so that it becomes increasingly obvious, Minister, that the Western democracies are on the verge of collapse. The way of life to which we have become accustomed will soon be a thing of the past. Failure to act decisively to this new set of global circumstances will have catastrophic consequences for all of our citizens. The nation is unable to rely on imports of gas, oil, coal and basic foodstuffs and ill-prepared to deal with their lack. And the scarcity of these resources will create social tensions that are the perfect incendiaries for civil unrest, if not all out civil war.

The only way forward is to make Britain self-sufficient. However, with the population currently standing at over 75 million, at least twice what the area or arable land is able to support,[1] we find ourselves in an untenable situation. Leading to one inevitable conclusion. Only Controlled Depopulation (CDP)

---

1 *Some studies suggest the UK is three times over its optimum population – see attached documents.*

will allow the country to survive in the immediate term, never mind into the second half of the century.

Again, my Dept. is forced to propose urgent action to rebalance the population and bring it within acceptable parameters. The draft legislation we shared with you last year must be put before the House during this sitting.

To recap the key points as follows:

The immediate expulsion of all non-nationals to their country of origin.

The enforced repatriation of all immigrants who are not entitled to British citizenship.

Rescinding of remaining treaties with European Confederation countries and the free movement of nationals between member nations that those treaties enshrine.

Licensed reproduction and the imposition of a one-child-only law on all UK citizens.

Enforced abortion of all embryos found to have birth defects or conceived without license.

Enforced sterilisation of criminals, vagrants, the unemployed and all other undesirables.

It is estimated that the immediate introduction of the above legislation will reduce our population by some 10 million within the first two years. And a further 14 million over the following five years. While this leaves us some way off the 40 million maximum which is commonly accepted the country can support it will, at least, give us a fighting chance.

Minister, in the best interests of the nation, I urge you to act. We cannot watch from the sidelines while catastrophe hurtles towards us when measures can be put in place now that can make a difference and secure the nation's future. Do nothing and history will judge us all.

Yours,
XXXREDACTEDXXX
Head of Research, Dept. of Internal Readiness.

PART I

A beach flooded with moonlight.

A teenager inches into the flickering circle of shadows cast by a driftwood fire. It's a girl but, at first glance, it would be hard to tell. Her hair is too short, and her face is too dirty to be certain.

Her mother might know her.

But her mother is dead.

In the background, the rhythmic churning sound of the sea. It's out there, of course it is, but it's too dark to see it.

The ragged people gathered at the fire shuffle sullenly around to make a little room for the newcomer, who nods in thanks, squats down on her haunches and peels off her gloves. She holds out her hands to the flames, rubbing them together as if washing them in the warmth.

With her, a dog. A half-starved and filthy looking thing. It walks a circle around her then sits down at her side, tongue lolling, eyes gleaming in the light of the fire.

Across from her a mother, shapeless under the layers of rags she's wearing, nudges the dirt-streaked child beside her. The child looks up. The mother reaches into a drawstring bag tied around her waist and, rooting around inside, pulls out a creased and greasy paper bag. She unfolds the scrunched-up end and, reaching in, extracts a lump of bread. She breaks a piece from one end, hands it to the child, and nods toward the newcomer. The child gets up, walks around the fire, and stands in front of the girl and her dog. The child holds out the bread at arm's length for the girl to take.

The girl looks at the child. Then at the mother. She takes the bread. The child dashes back to the safety of her mother's side.

The newcomer nods to the woman in gratitude and starts to eat.

Wolfishly.
One bite.
Two bites.
Gone.

Then she looks around the sea of sad, fire-lit faces. They are all similarly streaked with dirt, hollow, prematurely old. But there is an urging in their eyes. She reaches into the cavernous pocket of her filthy overcoat and produces a battered plastic bottle, removes the lid, takes a few sips to wash down the dry, stale bread and screws the lid tightly back into place. The bottle is immediately returned to the pocket.

She clears her throat and starts to speak…

1

Apart from the street where I lived and the infant school I went to, I don't remember much about St Albans. Which is to be expected, I suppose. I was very young, and it was a long time ago. (For all I know, St Albans isn't even there anymore.)

But I remember every detail of the night we left.

At least, I think I do.

(Memory's a funny thing and can sometimes play tricks on you.)

I was six years old.

At the first squeak of the door handle my eyes sprang open. I watched it slowly turn, the door ease open, light spill in from the landing. The gap between the bottom of the bedroom door and the carpet wasn't quite big enough which meant that, every time it opened or closed, there was an accompanying 'whooshing' sound.

(I loved the warm thickness of that carpet on my bare feet. Used to scrunch up my toes and wriggle them around in it.)

A silhouette was framed in the doorway, backlit by the landing light. I closed my eyes tight again and pretended to be asleep while they tiptoed across the room and drew down the covers. Then carefully, like someone carrying a bundle of wet washing, they scooped me up in their arms.

I'd always been a light sleeper, I still am, so no matter how quietly Dad tried to sneak in, he was always going to wake me. He wasn't a very affectionate man, my dad. He could be quite remote. Which meant that cuddles were rare and all the more precious for that.

A special birthday hug.

Sitting on his lap on Christmas morning while I unwrapped presents.

A congratulatory cuddle for a drawing brought home from school with a gold star from Miss Taylor on it.

My mum more than made up for any lack. She always did the tucking in, told the bedtime story, delivered the final goodnight kiss. But, as far as I knew (and I was a very light sleeper), this was the first time Dad had ever come into my room while I was asleep. I looped my arms around his neck and worked my head into the comfortable dip between his neck and collarbone. I nestled into the wool of his gardening jumper like a hamster, enjoying its musty, fusty, garden smell. (Why was he wearing that?) Lost in the mix of smells, drowsy with sleep, warm and protected, I think I was as happy as I'd ever been.

Because of that, it didn't occur to me to wonder *why* he was in my room in the dead of night, picking me up and carrying me away from the delicious cocoon of my bed.

I was spirited out of the room, down the stairs, through the open front door of our house and straight outside, the chilly air gripping me, to the waiting camper van.

All in absolute silence.

Another drowsy peek and I glimpsed my mother standing by the open passenger door and my two older brothers, Rich and Tom, peering out through the van's side windows. They were yawning, cavernously.

Dad carefully set me down in the double-width passenger

seat, wrapped the seatbelt around me and clicked it into place. Mum slid in alongside, her smells so different to his: perfume and soap, comfort and cleanliness. She wrapped an arm around my shoulders and my head lolled against her side, seeking out the comfort of her body's warmth.

"Where are we going?" I mumbled.

"On an adventure," she said.

And with that, I was back under again. Just the play of headlights flashing yellows and reds across the curtain of my eyelids. And then the sweet, deep oblivion of childhood sleep.

If I'd known then that it would be the last time I'd ever see my bedroom with the Snow White wallpaper (I'd chosen it myself), the house that was my entire world, the street that seemed as big as the universe, I might have paid a little more attention.

Given it a parting look.

Watched it ebb into the distance as we pulled out of the drive.

I might also have been inconsolable.

Which is, I expect, precisely why my parents chose to do it like this. To take flight in the middle of the night like thieves while the rest of the world was sleeping.

2

When I woke up, we were far away from home. Mum's voice cut through the blanket of sleep I'd wrapped myself up in, her hand gently stroking my face while she sang out my name.

"A-lice. A-lice. Time to wake up now."

Opening my eyes, Mum's face filled the earth and sky.

"Are we there?"

"Not yet, my lovely. We're stopping for a break."

I looked around while she undid the seatbelt and pulled me toward the van's open door. This place was wholly new to me. Of course, I'd seen more than city streets even by the age of six. We'd taken family holidays to beaches and woodlands and my dad, a big fan of the Sunday walk, would drive us out into the country for rambles. But this was unlike any of those pleasant, neat, recreational places. On either side of the ribbon of grey road, gorse and heather stretched to the horizon, occasionally interrupted by the bumps and bruises of exposed boulders.

A light drizzle was falling and, with the door of the van open, I could see my breath in the morning air.

"It's cold," I said.

My mum, two steps ahead, was ready with a warm jacket and teased my unresisting arms into the sleeves before shoving my feet into my pride and joy – a pair of red, polka-dot wellies.

She held me under the arms and helped me down from the van.

Dad had pulled into a layby with a few picnic tables and a toilet block. My brothers were already standing by the roadside in zipped-up parkas, their arms folded tightly across their chests and their hands tucked into their armpits. They had wellies on as well and stepped from foot to foot, blowing out clouds of warm breath and watching me blankly as Mum lead me past them to the loo.

They were both older than me, but Tom was the oldest, although only by ten months. This made them 'Irish twins' according to Dad. Tom was a head taller than Rich but skinny, while Rich was stocky. Tom was the one who always wanted to play, tickle, chase, so I had more fun with him. But it was Rich who always knew if I was sad and would do his best to cheer me up when I was worried about something.

They'd both been bored rigid in the camper van, which had none of the in-car entertainment we were used to. We'd had a people carrier with seat-back monitors, a choice of games, channels and internet, but Mum and Dad had sold it months earlier and replaced it with this camper thing. A bark from Dad soon got them moving.

"Oi, you two, help me with this."

Dad was carrying a large, plastic cool box. The boys sullenly trudged towards him, and he handed it over.

On my return from the bathroom, the contents of the cooler were laid out on one of the picnic tables. There was bread, jam, plastic cups of juice. Dad was standing at the side of the road holding a cup of coffee, peering back in the direction we'd come, talking into a mobile phone. As he spoke, he stood on tiptoe and craned his neck. I watched over a slice of Mother's Pride white with a thick layer of strawberry jam that Mum had spread for me. Suddenly, Dad started to wave back down the road. A large, white van appeared some distance away, getting rustier as it got closer. He directed it into the layby and went around to the driver's side.

The engine stopped, the door swung open and out hopped Uncle Nick. He shook Dad's hand, both looking happy and relieved.

I smiled too, from ear to ear, talking around my jam sandwich.

"Look, Mum, it's Nuncle."

"Yes, honey. Yes it is."

My infant tongue hadn't been able to separate the words 'uncle' and 'Nick', running them into one another to create the name 'Nuncle'. Of course, my brothers thought this was hilarious and mimicked me every time I did it, repeating the word 'Nuncle, Nuncle' in sing-song voices. Originality was never their strong suit so today was no different.

"Nuncle, Nuncle." They laughed, showing off bits of jam and bread between their teeth. Mum hushed them up before I had a chance to get upset.

Dad and Nick had finished the handshaking and my uncle handed over his phone. I watched, not really understanding, while Dad dismantled them both, took out the chips and smashed all the bits with a rock. Then he scooped up the pieces and threw them into one of the overflowing bins. Meanwhile, Nuncle helped his wife, Flick, down from the van. She looked tired from the journey, smiled a weak smile and gave my dad a peck on the cheek. They came over to the picnic table, Mum standing up as they approached. A slightly nervous look had crept into her eyes. She tucked her hair back behind her ears and ran one hand under her chin, before clasping them both together in front of her.

"Julia!" Nick smiled, giving her a peck on both cheeks.

"Hello, Nick. Hello, Felicity." She accepted Nick's kiss and then shook Felicity's hand.

"Hello, Julia."

Nick looked around at the rest of us. "Hello, trouble," he said to my brothers.

They smiled back at him. They liked being thought of as troublemakers.

"And how's my little Alice?"

"I'm very well, thank you, Nuncle." Again, laughter from my brothers, which Dad silenced with a glare.

I had deployed my best grown-up phrase; one Mum had taught me to use when introduced to visitors and special people. To me, there was no one more special than Uncle Nick. Hugs were never rationed with him, and his sense of fun was infectious. Even my dad was less serious and somehow lighter when his younger brother was around. Nick looked quickly around the breakfast table, assessing the situation.

"We're starving, aren't we, Felicity? What's for breakfast?"

"Bread and jam," said Tom sullenly.

"There's nothing wrong with a bit of bread and jam, is there, Flick?" Nick rubbed his hands together as he spoke, warming them up and at the same time creating the impression that a breakfast feast awaited him.

"You can have mine if you like." I held up the remains of my jam sandwich for him. This earned me a hug, which is why I offered it in the first place.

"That's all right, munchkin, I wouldn't steal your breakfast. I can make my own. Budge up."

He squeezed in next to me on the bench, Felicity took the spot opposite him, and he started buttering bread.

My dad had still to eat too, and he pushed the boys out of the way to make room. "Any trouble on the road?" he asked Nick as he refilled his coffee cup from a thermos.

"A few roadblocks in Sheffield." He cast a more serious look towards Felicity. "We had to come off the M1 after that, didn't we."

She nodded.

"Burned-out cars. Impassable. Directed off at Junction 34, weaved our way up on the A-roads. Thank God I've got a good map reader." He gave Felicity a nudge and she smiled back at him.

"I never liked GPS," she said. "Some awful robot woman in your car telling you where to go. I always preferred a real map so, you know, I don't miss it."

Nuncle and Flick had been married for a year or so. I was a flower girl at their wedding. I had no memory of the previous girlfriends Nick had introduced to the family, but my brothers did. When Nick first brought Felicity to meet us, Rich had 'accidentally' (or so he claimed between sobs afterwards as Dad gave him the tongue-lashing of the century) called her by the name of one of Nick's exes. Felicity took this in her stride, throwing in a few childhood embarrassments that Rich had suffered by way of revenge. Stories about bed-wettings, first kisses, that kind of thing. Stuff that I would never have learned about otherwise and which Nuncle must have armed her with in advance. I liked her immediately.

"How are you doing for petrol?" asked Dad.

"Not quite running on empty yet," said Nuncle. "You could see the gauge going down before your eyes on some of those hills. But we've been saving our ration for months now and there's enough spare in the cans to get us there... I hope. How about your holiday home?"

This got a grin out of Dad. "We should be okay, even with all the dead weight we're carrying in the back." He darted a quick look left and right at his two boys.

Rich, yawning around a mouthful of jam sandwich, asked, "So where are we going anyway?"

The adults looked at one another for a moment and, without speaking, came to a decision. Dad reached inside his jacket and pulled out a road map. "You two, move some of these things out of the way."

My brothers cleared the table and Dad laid the map out flat, using the palm of his hand to smooth out the wrinkles. We all leaned in. I stood up on the seat for a better look, Nuncle's hand supporting me in the small of my back. While everyone else seemed excited, to me it was all a complication of colours, shapes and lines. I looked at the map, frowning deeply, imagining that if I stared at it hard enough, I might be able to make sense of it.

Then Dad spoke. "We're going to Scotland."

"Scotland?" they said, pretty much in unison. The boys looked at him, intrigued, and I followed their lead.

Dad poked at finger at the unfolded road map. "We're here, about an hour short of the border. After breakfast, we'll head off in the camper and make the crossing." His finger started to shape a route along one of the map's multitude of lines, the colour of the land either side changing from light green to dark brown as the finger weaved its way north. "Then we go along here, and then here, here and, eventually, arrive here."

"The middle of nowhere," said Tom.

"Pretty much," Nuncle replied.

"But that's miles," said Rich. "How long's it going to take?"

"Another day… or so," was Dad's answer. "If we don't run out of petrol. Or have any trouble on the road."

"Call this a holiday? Two days cooped up in that old van, with nothing to do?" said Tom.

"We could have flown to Australia by now," added Rich. "And we've still got to schlep all the way home again afterwards."

The table fell silent, even Tom and Rich able to sense that whatever was about to come was going to be very important.

After a minute that stretched into forever, Dad spoke.

"We're not going back home." His finger made an emphatic stab at the map. "We've got a new home. Here."

The boys looked at each other, bewildered. But to me, too little to grasp the importance, it simply seemed like an extension of the adventure mum had promised me earlier. "You mean, we're going on holiday forever?"

"That's the spirit, munchkin," Nuncle said and put his arm around my shoulder, giving me a special Nuncle hug. The best hugs of all.

3

The rusty white van followed us for a few miles and then took a right turn. Nuncle and Flick gave us a wave which we all returned.

"Aren't they coming with us?" I asked Mum.

"They're taking a different road. We're going to meet them there."

"It's sort of a race," Dad explained.

Disappointed, I turned around in the passenger seat and kept waving until the van disappeared from sight.

In the back, Tom and Rich were entertaining themselves playing dead arms. The winner was the one who could be punched the hardest at the top of the arm without crying out in pain. Eventually, Rich made a whimper and Tom loudly proclaimed himself the winner.

"You two, keep it down," said Dad.

There were resentful huffs and puffs from behind us.

"Are we supposed to sit here in silence 'til we get there?" asked Tom. Then, eagerly, "Hey, Mum, did you pack my console?"

Rich chimed in, "Yeah, and mine."

"Sorry, boys, we didn't bring them."

They both fell silent. A simmering, angry silence. Rich whispered something to Tom, who took up their joint cause.

"We're moving to Scotland, like, forever and you forgot to bring our games consoles?"

"We didn't 'forget'," said Dad.

"So you left them behind on purpose?" asked Tom, outraged. "What's wrong with you?"

Dad's nostrils flared. "There'll be something wrong with you if you talk to me like that again."

Mum, ever the peacemaker, cut in. "Listen, we didn't forget them, we left them behind…" Tom and Rich started babbling over her but she ignored them and kept going. "Because, where we're moving to, there's no internet, no Wi-Fi, so your games wouldn't even work. Also, we're going to have to generate our own power and can't waste it on things like games because we'll need it for heating and lighting, important things like that."

They were both about a million miles away from happy about this. "You'll be telling me next that you left our phones as well," grumbled Tom.

Mum took a deep breath. "Actually, yes, we did leave your phones. There won't be enough power to keep recharging them and, the moment you switch them on, anyone can find out where you are."

Rich sounded genuinely distressed. "But what about our friends? How are we supposed to contact them?"

"We're starting a new life. You'll make new friends," said Mum, gently as she could.

The silence that descended now was thick and bitter. Eventually, Dad broke it. "We could have a sing-song?" he suggested hopefully.

"Are we going back in time as well as moving to the middle of nowhere?" Clearly, Rich had already had enough.

My father's knuckles tightened on the steering wheel and his jaw clenched. Mum reached across me to give him a squeeze on the shoulder. Then she turned around in her seat.

"Look in the second drawer down under the stove. There are some books about where we're moving to. You can make rope swings and tree houses, swim in the rivers, get lost in the woods. You'll love it... once you get used to it."

They dug out the books and started flicking through them, listlessly at first, but they were soon absorbed by images of giant stags, golden eagles and all the wild places. It made a change from seeing them glued to a phone or tablet.

"Are you bored too, my lovely?" she asked me.

I wasn't. I was happy staring out of the windows at the steep-sided valley the road was cutting through, alternating on either side between fields full of sheep and lambs, and densely wooded areas of dark pines.

"What's that?" I asked, pointing out an object at the edge of a field up ahead.

Dad was concentrating on driving, Mum gazing into the middle distance. They both looked towards the spot indicated by my outstretched finger. The shape was coming closer now, resolving into a ragged, human-like figure. It was close to the road in an approaching field, its spread-eagled limbs pinned to a makeshift wooden cross.

"Oh, that's just a scarecrow, honey," said Mum.

The arc of the road brought our camper van closer to the figure as we drove past. I'd seen scarecrows before, in books and, of course, in *The Wizard of Oz*. Scarecrows were stuffed with straw, their heads made out of a sack or, if you were in America, a pumpkin or something. Often they were dressed up in old suits, usually too short for them so that the wrists and ankles showed, with a piece of knotted string for a belt.

But this scarecrow was naked.

And he certainly wasn't scaring any crows.

Quite the opposite, he seemed to attract them. Black-feathered birds perched on the top of his head, shoulders and along the length of his outstretched arms, taking occasional pecks at him and throwing back their heads, beaks open, in order to swallow.

It was a man, bloated and misshapen, but definitely a man. Even aged six, I was certain of it. On a hand-scrawled sign hanging from a piece of string around his neck, someone had scrawled two words: 'No Passport'.

Mum's face was ashen. My dad's a grim shade of grey. He tried to squeeze out a reassuring smile for me but it was more like a grimace and that only made things worse. "Just a scarecrow, Alice, nothing to worry about." His eyes had a glassy, faraway look. In the back the boys were peering out of the window, mouths hanging open like fish, the picture books dead in their hands.

Around the next bend a large sign announced: 'Border 100 Yards – Slow Down'. This was nothing like the roads signs at home, neat metal circles and triangles with black silhouettes or big numbers printed on them. This was more like the graffiti we'd arrived at school one morning to find all over the classroom walls: streaks of red paint disfiguring the walls and running to the floor, the hasty daub of cruel and unskilled hands.

"Put the books away now, boys," said Dad. Rich and Tom did so instantly. Dad had slowed the camper van to a crawl. "Now, when we get to the border, be quiet and let me and your mum do the talking."

The road we were driving on was narrow, made narrower on the border approach by burned out and abandoned vehicles littering either side. Some still smouldered. Others had black, round puncture holes. All had shattered windscreens. I thought I saw a charcoal figure gripping the steering wheel of one, but the windscreen was shattered so I might have imagined it. Still, Mum put her arm around me and gently, but forcefully, turned my head so that my eyes faced front.

A sense of dread descended on us.

Slung across the road up ahead was a makeshift barrier flanked by guard boxes. As we approached at a snail's pace, a combat-dressed soldier emerged and approached us, signalling with his arm for us to stop. Dad brought the van to a gentle halt, turned off the engine and wound down his window. The soldier walked up alongside us and peered into the front and back of the camper.

"Morning, Officer," said Dad, trying to reassure us that he, at least, knew what he was doing.

"Passports please, sir."

Do you remember, before barcodes there were these things called 'passports'? Little printed books with your name, photo and date of birth in them. It seems silly now that a little book could be used to prove to someone else who you were. I mean, what was to stop you from making your own? But people were more trusting then. And the world was safer.

Mum reached into the glove compartment, dug out our documents and handed them across to Dad, who duly handed them on to the soldier. In the meantime, three more soldiers had come out from the guard boxes, weapons levelled on the front of our van.

The first soldier flicked through the passports, holding them up on the photo page and staring intently at each one of us in turn. "Five of you travelling, correct?" He had a Scottish accent, which I'd not heard before except on TV.

"Yes, sir."

"Reason for travel?"

"Visiting relatives. I wanted to get my kids away from the city, get some fresh air in their lungs."

The soldier put our passports into his jacket pocket and held out his hand. "Keys, please, sir."

"Wha... what?"

"Can I have the keys to the vehicle please, sir."

It wasn't a request, it was an order. Dad shot a glance at Mum, who looked back at him, pleading with her eyes for him not to hand the keys over. This small hesitation was all it took for the soldier to repeat the instruction.

"If I have to ask a third time, sir, you will be putting yourself and your family in extreme jeopardy."

Dad reached forward and took the keys from the ignition, fighting a tremor in his right hand. He gave them to the soldier who snatched them away.

"Thank you, sir. If you would all remain inside the vehicle."

The soldier strode back to the guard box while his three compatriots remained in position, guns still trained on us. I watched the senior officer in the booth, holding up each passport and examining it closely, running what looked like a torchlight over each one. Next to me, Mum's body was rigid, all trace of softness gone.

"Adam?" she said under her breath, lips barely parting.

"What?" Dad hissed back at her, eyes trained on the three armed men guarding the vehicle.

"Adam, look at me."

He flashed her a furious look. "Now is not the time."

The officer emerged from the booth and walked back towards us, passports in hand. He spoke to one of his unit, who accompanied him to the driver's side window, weapon poised. I noticed that beads of sweat had formed on Dad's forehead.

The officer reached in through the window and handed the passports back to Dad. "Here you are, sir." He gestured up the road. "Enjoy your holiday." The officer even managed a thin smile as he looked at each of us in turn.

"Tha… thank you," Dad stammered.

"May I recommend that you choose a different crossing point for your return trip?"

Dad was already nodding, eagerly.

"As you can see, we've had a spot of bother here. This route is favoured by illegals, terrorists, all sorts. I'd suggest a nice, white family like you find a different way home."

"Of course. Thanks, thanks very much, Officer."

One of the soldiers approached the barrier and raised it for us, while the officer waved us on through and took a few steps back from the window.

"The key?"

"Sorry, sir?"

"The key," Dad repeated. "You still have it."

"Oh, of course. I was forgetting."

The officer reached into his trouser pocket, produced the camper van key on its Eiffel Tower keyring, and passed it through the window.

Dad retrieved it, put it into the ignition, and turned. The engine gunned and he released the handbrake. The camper van lurched forward, then came to a juddering halt. We all rocked first forward and then back in our seats. I'd never known him stall a car before.

He took a deep breath and tried again.

Switched off the engine.

Turned the key.

Started the van and, this time, pulled away serenely, under the raised barrier and over the border into Scotland.

After that, for a long time, we drove on in silence.

4

We drove all day, Scotland rattling past in the camper van's windows.

When I wasn't dozing, I was entranced. Back home everything had been safe, predictable and boring. Boxy houses on little streets and, beyond them, orderly fields separated by wooden fences. Now I watched, thrilled, as mountains and valleys, forests and rivers, advanced towards us and receded behind. I saw a dozen different shades of brown, green and red. Even the road signs were exciting, promising rock falls and leaping stags. Perhaps I would have felt differently if we'd been driving through bad weather but spring was being kind; the sun shone, the sky was a perfect blue.

We skirted the towns when we could – Selkirk, Peebles, Stirling – and kept heading relentlessly north. We took meal breaks at picnic spots. Clambering down from the camper and stretching my little legs, I think I breathed properly for the very first time. The air was alive with smells I didn't recognise but have since learned to love. Resinous pine and burnished wood. My head reeled, intoxicated by it, like the first time I downed scrumpy straight from the barrel. Even the trauma of the border crossing started to recede.

It took much longer than Dad had thought to reach our new

home. Dark had long since come and the smooth, tarmacked road we'd been driving on had been replaced by a surface rutted and uneven. I was shaken awake by the bumps and, disorientated, looked around. In every direction, there was only blackness.

"Are we there yet?" I asked Mum sleepily.

"Not long now, dear."

Behind me, Tom and Rich were comatose, stretched out on the built-in sofas on either side of the van. Tom was snoring like a foghorn.

Dad peered out of the front window, intently following the twin beams of the van's headlamps. I craned my neck over the dashboard for a look. Ahead of us, a wall of trees suddenly appeared and Dad flung the steering wheel to the left and drove on, keeping the trees on the van's right-hand side.

The road surface became even bumpier, throwing me up and down as the camper van's old bones struggled to cope. Dad turned the steering wheel sharply to the right, through a gap in the wall of trees. We were flung sideways and suddenly driving up a steep incline. The tone of the engine changed, struggling with the terrain, Dad fighting with the gear stick and grinding through the gears as we crawled ever upwards. Then we were descending again and I could see the muddy, rutted path in the bouncing headlights.

The road evened out and looking further, beyond the twin beams, I caught a glimpse of light. Flickering on and off at first, but then steady.

And coming closer.

Then a second light at the same distance as the first.

Moments later, I made out a shape: the vague outline of a building.

A house.

Lit from within. And Nuncle and Flick's rusty white van parked up outside it.

At last, we were here.

Dad brought the camper to a slow stop, turned off the engine and leaned back in his seat. He closed his eyes, pushed his glasses up onto his forehead and rubbed the bridge of his nose. He took a long, deep breath, held it in, and then let it out again slowly. He let his glasses slide back down into place and looked across at Mum. He smiled, relieved. She smiled back.

"We're here, honey," she said and rubbed the top of my head.

Nuncle and Flick appeared in the doorway. They had their pyjamas on with big, warm parkas over the top, were carrying torches and wearing wellies. Dad waved and hopped out of the van. Mum followed his lead, helping me down behind her.

In St Albans our house had been on a street of other houses exactly like it, joined to the one next door, all built of identical red bricks. This was a three-storey building made of cream-coloured stone blocks, each one nearly the size of me. It stood alone, far away from any other houses, isolated for miles in every direction by fields and woods. The van's bright headlights reflected back off black windows that stared like lidless eyes while the bobbing torches created an ever-shifting landscape of light and dark. I peered up toward the top of the building and nearly toppled over but could make out a sharply pointed roof against the night sky.

Dad slid open the van's side door and, leaning in, roughly shook Tom and Rich awake. "Oi, you two, wake up. We're here."

They peeled open their eyes and, in a zombie-like trance, staggered out into the frigid night air. Rich, a fraction more with it than Tom, had the presence of mind to look around and ask in a barely audible whisper, "And where the Hell *is* here?" This earned him a shove from Dad in the direction of the open front door, a rectangle of light in the inky dark.

I stood holding Mum's hand but, having been bounced awake on the approach to the farm, I was suddenly overwhelmed by tiredness. I felt it rushing over me like a warm wave, up my feet, past my knees until my head was bobbing. I leaned my head back and yawned, tottering backwards. But Nuncle was on hand and, in a single motion, scooped me up in his arms.

"There you go, munchkin, I've got you." He looked over at Mum. "It's okay, I'll take her."

"Thanks, Nick."

He carried me into the house past Flick, who watched from under hooded eyes, arms folded tightly across her chest. Mum followed us in and Flick slammed the door shut behind her.

I'd left my old home in the arms of Dad and entered my new one in the arms of Nuncle. As my head lolled I was carried upstairs into the bedroom. I was put into the big, old bed and, as Mum tucked me in, I noticed the opposite wall was decorated with the same Snow White wallpaper from my bedroom in St Albans.

The effect was confusing.

Disorientating.

Was this my old room or a new one?

"Am I at home?" I asked her.

She smiled indulgently.

"Yes, hon. Your new home," she said and kissed my forehead. "Sleep now, it's very late." She retreated back through the open door and closed it after her.

Then sleep took me.

5

That first night the Scarecrow came to visit me.

Back in the old house, in my old room, there had been a clock shaped like a cartoon mouse, whose hands glowed in the dark and pointed to the time. I had a nightlight, too. And there was always some light spilling in through the curtains from the streetlamps outside, from the headlights of passing cars, or snaking in around the bedroom door.

But here there was nothing.

The room was so dark that at first it was impossible to work out whether I was awake or still sleeping.

I had no clue what had disturbed me, didn't know how long I'd been asleep or what woke me from it. Certainly, no one had come into my new bedroom through the creaky old door. I would have heard that, for certain.

As my eyes slowly adjusted to the darkness I could make out the characters on my wallpaper. Dark blobs against the white background began to resolve into the familiar shapes of Snow White, her friends the dwarves, and the woodland creatures she played with.

There she was, balancing a robin on her outstretched finger.

Next to that, gathering the dwarves around her and hugging even the grumpiest of them.

Next, holding an apple offered to her by a wizened old crone.

But there was a section of the wall where it was impossible to make out any pattern. Where the princess and her friends didn't become clearer the longer I stared at them.

A part of the wall obscured by shadow.

I stared into the shadow. And the shadow stared back.

I held my breath as the shadow took shape.

A ragged, misshapen figure shuffled out of it.

The Scarecrow.

The one I'd seen crucified in the field before the border crossing.

Even in the dark I knew it.

My heart hammered in my chest. It had never hammered so hard before. An angry, booted foot kicking at a locked and bolted door, intent on bursting it open.

It hammered in my ears.

It hammered behind my eyes.

It hammered so loud he must have been able to hear it.

The Scarecrow's hulking mass stepped out from the safety of the shadows and inched towards my bed.

I knew him by the blackness of his skin.

By the sheets of flesh torn from his shoulders.

By his nakedness.

He had climbed down from his crude cross, unpicked the nails and barbed wire that held him in place, and followed me here.

I held my breath.

I didn't cry out.

I don't know why.

Perhaps because, in all the stories I'd seen or read that had a scarecrow in them, the scarecrow always came to life. So it didn't seem odd to me that this scarecrow, stuck in a field by the side of a road, suffering the indignity of crows, might choose to follow me here.

He inched towards my bed. Slowly. Stealthily. I felt his weight as he sat down on the foot of it. He was silent for a minute that stretched into two, the ruined shape of a man, perched uncomfortably at the foot of my bed. I held my breath, heartbeats thundering in my ears. His ruined face inched around towards me and I saw that the crows had been busy there, too, because he had no eyes to meet mine.

Then he spoke.

Not out loud.

Not using his lips. (The crows had taken care of them as well.)

But I heard his sandpaper voice inside my head as clearly as if he were talking to me. A nursery rhyme, a favourite of mine because it was one of the few Dad sang to me. And, just as Dad did, the Scarecrow changed the word 'mama' to 'daddy'.

Hush little baby, don't say a word,
Daddy's gonna buy you a mockingbird,
And if that mockingbird don't sing,
Daddy's gonna buy you a diamond ring,
And if that diamond ring turns brass,
Daddy's gonna buy you a looking glass.
And if that looking glass gets broke,
Daddy's gonna...

...buy you a nanny goat? That's how it ends, isn't it?

No. Not this time.

Not in the Scarecrow's version.

On the last line he lurched up the bed towards me, leaning over me so that his face and mine were only millimetres apart. I could see the full horror of his ruined face, his lipless mouth, his empty eye sockets. The voice in my head, clear as a cracked bell...

Daddy's gonna tie a noose round your throat.

And then I did cry out.

I screamed and screamed and screamed and screamed.

The bedroom door was flung open and at the flick of a switch the bare electric light bulb instantly banished the apparition. I was still screaming as Mum strode into the room, knelt beside the bed and threw hers arms around me. Behind her, a moment later, Dad appeared, hovering anxiously in the doorway.

"Sshhh, sshhh, there, there, Alice. Everything's okay." She rocked me gently back and forth. My screams began to subside along with my heart rate. Mum sat down on the bed, where moments before the Scarecrow had been. She rested a hand on mine and gave it a squeeze. "Bad dream, darling?"

I'd had bad dreams before, of course I had, but this was something else.

Much more vivid.

Much more real.

I nodded just the same.

"It's okay," she said, "it's to be expected. Such a big change." Her face was etched with worry.

By now I was feeling calmer and managed a thin smile, more for Mum's sake than my own. "You gonna be okay now, hon?" I nodded. She stood and Dad put his arm around her shoulders, gave her a hug, and they both gave me concerned looks. "Okay well, if you need us, we're just down the corridor. And Nuncle and Flick are in the room opposite."

"So you're completely surrounded by people who love you," Dad added. "Okay?"

"Okay."

"All right then. Goodnight, Alice."

"Goodnight." Dad drew Mum reluctantly away.

As his hand hovered over the light switch I said, "Dad?"

"Yes?"

"Can you leave the light on please?"

"Of course." He withdrew his hand from the switch.

They left and quietly closed the door behind them.

It was weeks before I could sleep at all without the electric light for company.

If only my Mickey Mouse nightlight had made the journey north with us.

6

The next morning, Mum tried to creep into my room but the squeaky bedroom door gave her away.

"What time is it?" I asked woozily as she tiptoed towards me.

"Breakfast time. Everyone else is already up. Did you sleep okay after we left?"

"I had a bad dream."

Was it a dream? That was the only explanation that made any sense. I was certain I'd been awake when the Scarecrow first appeared, that Mum and Dad hadn't woken me up when they came in, more that they'd scared the Scarecrow off.

But it must have been a bad dream. What else could it be?

"I know. Don't worry about it, baby." She stroked the hair from my forehead. "It's all so new and the journey took so long. You're bound to be unsettled." She leaned towards me and planted a kiss on the tip of my nose. It made me giggle. "Quick now, or the boys will eat the lot."

I was led downstairs where, as this was the first family meal in our new home, she and Flick had gone to extra effort and prepared an enormous spread. Tom and Rich were tucking into slices of bread and jam on top of the cereal and boiled eggs they'd already polished off. But Mum needn't have worried, there was still plenty left for me.

"Here she is, sleeping beauty," said Tom. I stuck my tongue out at him and narrowed my eyes viciously.

"Now, Tom, Alice was awake a lot longer than you last night. She made sure we got here safely, didn't you, honey?"

I nodded superiorly. Mum helped me up onto the tallest of the mismatched chairs around the table and put my plastic breakfast bowl with the pale blue stripe, the only bowl I'd eat from, down in front of me.

"Shreddies?"

Emphatic nodding. Shreddies were my favourite.

I looked around the table as I ate. It was large enough to comfortably accommodate the whole extended family. Its surface was a dark, rough wood, with an interesting patchwork of stains. The kitchen floor was smooth-scrubbed stone, cold on your toes first thing in the morning (I soon learned not to enter the kitchen barefoot), the walls a dull green that would soon be coated bright yellow. Against the far wall was a large cooking range, and a metal sink under the big window looked out onto the back garden.

Dad and Nuncle came in from outside, accompanied by a cold draft of morning air.

"She's up then?" said Dad with a grin.

"Morning, munchkin," added Nuncle. He helped himself to a slice of buttered toast from a plate piled high in the centre of the table and went over to Flick, who was nursing a large mug of coffee. He gave her a quick peck on top of the head.

"And how's Mrs Fox feeling now?"

"Still waiting for the caffeine to work its magic."

"So what's the plan then, Dad?" asked Tom.

"Well, once we've all finished breakfast, we're going to go out and explore the farm. There's loads to show you and lots to do. But the hard work won't start 'til tomorrow."

The boys' faces fell at the first mention of 'work', a dirty word whatever came before it, whether 'school', 'home' or 'house'. But 'hard' work? That was the dirtiest word of all.

"There are laws against child labour, you know," said Rich.

"Fair enough. But if you don't work, you don't eat."

"Oh, Adam," said Mum sharply before adding, more softly, to my brothers, "We live together as a family, we work together as a family. That's how it has to be now."

"So we've got to work here all hours and fit in school too? This is balls. I want to go home," said Tom, pushing his plate away and emphatically folding his arms across his chest.

"This *is* home. The old house is sold. There's nothing to go back to," Dad replied, his voice rising.

Mum stepped in. "We don't expect you to work here and go to school as well. So… you're not going to school."

My brothers' eyes widened. "No school?" It was a difficult idea for them to grasp. But Tom grasped it first.

"*Cool!*"

The grown-ups smiled but I wasn't nearly so pleased. I liked school and was good at my schoolwork. I liked it when Miss Taylor, who was always very kind, put a gold star on my spelling test or told us how well we'd done. I liked being clever and didn't want to fall behind.

"There'll be classes in the morning with me and Flick, so you'll still be learning," Mum explained.

"But given there are only three of you and two of us giving lessons, you should learn twice as much in half the time," added Flick. "When I was a teaching assistant with a class of forty to look after, it was more like riot control than education."

Of course. Flick had been a teacher in London before the schools there had been closed down. She knew what to do.

"Schools only fill your head with rubbish and lies. Here, you'll learn what you need to. How to grow things, how to survive. Now, eat up everyone, time to get moving." Dad was eager to get the day underway.

"We've not showered yet," said Rich.

"Oh, I wouldn't worry too much about that, son. You'll only get mucky again once you're outside. You can wash before dinner."

No school and no washing? If my brothers' faces were anything to go by, life on the farm suddenly seemed a whole lot brighter.

I gobbled the last of my Shreddies and Mum took me upstairs to brush my teeth and pick some outdoor clothes from the piles of bags littering the bedroom floor. Ten minutes later, we were back downstairs and ready to commence day one of our new lives.

7

As far as my parents were concerned, the fewer people who knew when or why we'd left St Albans, the better.

Which explained the midnight flit and leaving at the start of the Easter break.

Anything to delay the awkward questions.

They hadn't even told my brothers, only too aware of a child's need to share a secret with a school friend. They could have been pretty confident that one of those friends would share the secret with an adult, who would start by asking questions and answer them by informing the authorities that Adam Fox and his wife Julia planned to take their children out of school for the foreseeable future.

Scratch that.

I mean 'forever'.

More than anything, they wanted complete secrecy about *where* we'd gone. Dad was convinced that petrol would soon go from a rationed luxury to something people would fight and kill for. At which point, escape would be impossible. My parents had watched food prices rise to a point where a lot of ordinary people weren't able to afford the basics. There had already been food riots and it didn't take a genius to work out that they would become more regular. And more desperate.

And then?

The overpopulated cities would burst open and spill out into the surrounding countryside. St Albans, and hundreds of small towns like it around London, would be pitifully unprepared to deal with whatever bitter, desperate and starving city dwellers were capable of.

You could sit and wait for it to happen or take your chances and get out.

My dad's vision was of a self-sufficient smallholding capable of supporting an extended family, as far from major cities as it's possible to get.

And that meant Scotland.

But how long would it be before more people had the same idea?

Once the end became obvious, the prices of small farmhouses with a couple of acres would sky-rocket as more and more frightened people literally headed for the hills.

So Dad reasoned, coaxed and ultimately browbeat Mum, Nuncle and Flick into sharing his vision and uprooted the family in search of a safe haven from the storm.

In all these things, he was proved right.

As we all now know, the worst did come to pass.

And all the darkness of the human soul was given free rein to express itself.

Including his own.

8

We started our first day with a tour of the farm buildings. The farmhouse, which I'd only glimpsed the previous night, was built in an L-shape, with an old bit that had been there for hundreds of years and a newer wing that had been added centuries later. On the first floor there five bedrooms, one for me, one for my brothers, one each for the adult couples and a spare, "In case we have any unexpected guests," said Nuncle, giving Flick a hug.

I didn't think we were likely to get many unexpected guests all the way out here.

But I was only six.

Me and my brothers took it in turns identifying our rooms from the outside and bickering about who had the best view. My room was at the front of the house and looked out across the garden, a large field and down the hill to the little stream that bordered the property, while the boys' room was at the back of the house and looked out onto the wooded hillside. I wouldn't have liked that as I'd have imagined creatures peering in at me from under the dark cover of the branches. Tom and Rich said that was exactly why they did like it.

One small window looked out from the very top floor. This was an attic room where Dad and Nuncle were going to install a generator.

"We bought a wind turbine with us in the back of the van," Nuncle explained. "We'll rig it up on the roof and that will give us enough electricity to power the lights and the freezer."

We continued the tour. There were a couple of run-down sheds with corrugated tin roofs in need of repair. Mum felt it was safer we didn't explore those. There was also a large, two-storey, stone-built barn. The previous owners had used it as a garage for their tractor and to store hay. "A bloody waste of something so solidly built," was how Dad put it.

Circling round to the front of the house, we followed an overgrown path to an old stone wall. An archway lead to a sheltered orchard, the mature trees laid out in neat rows. Dead branches littered the weed-filled grass.

"Apple and pear trees," said Nuncle. "Twenty of each. They haven't been taken good care of but a bit of TLC, saw off a few dead limbs, root out the creepers, and we should get a good crop." He scooped me up under the arms and held me over his head, giving me a closer look at the nearest tree. I let out a giggle. "Imagine it, munchkin. Apple pie galore!" Nuncle span me around a couple of times and then placed me back down in the ankle-deep weeds. The world whirred around me for a couple of seconds. "And enough left over for cider making, eh, boys?" Tom and Rich giggled now.

Exiting the orchard, Dad lead us across the lawn at the front of the house, over a low wall and out into a ploughed field where the earth had been churned into rows of clayey ruts. "We paid the farmer across the valley to plough it for us, so we're all set for the first year," said Dad, proud of his planning.

"What are we going to grow?" asked Tom.

"Potatoes. Easiest crop in the world. Throw them into the ground, stand back and leave them to it. What we can't eat, we'll sell. What we can't sell we'll feed to the pigs. Keep some seed potatoes back for next year and repeat the cycle."

"Pigs?" It was my turn to pipe up.

Nuncle took over. "Absolutely. Little porkers, dozens of them running around. We're turning one of the old sheds into a sty. Pigs will eat anything, live off our scraps. We'll have bangers and mash for tea every night, with apple sauce from our own orchard. I'm getting hungry just thinking about it."

"There'll be chickens too. A good layer produces an egg a day," said Mum. "We plan to have a dozen, so there'll always be eggs for breakfast and extras for baking."

"A century of female emancipation and look at us now, back in the kitchen," said Flick.

Nuncle laughed. "While the men are in the fields breaking their backs. I think I'd rather be in the warm kitchen where the food is." He slipped an arm around her waist.

At the far end of the field was a narrow strip of trees, then the stream. A path ran parallel with the stream before bending to the right and out of sight. "This leads to the village, takes a while to walk there but we'll still need supplies. And I thought we could go to church this Sunday, as it's Easter, put in an appearance."

This made me happy. I was sure there'd be children of my own age in the village and might make some new friends to make up for the ones I'd left behind.

We swung back towards the farmhouse and Mum explained her plans for a vegetable garden. "It's just an overgrown patch of grass and weeds right now but spring's the perfect time for planting. I want to grow cabbages and carrots, peas and parsnips, and tomato plants and lettuces might grow too, if the weather's kind."

"We have to make sure we get our five a day," Nuncle added cheerily.

"And in the autumn we'll raid the hedgerows for berries and make jam for winter," said Mum.

Dad had led us back to the parked vans. "Enough chat, time to unpack." He threw open the sliding door to the camper while Nuncle freed the chain and padlock securing the back of his rusty old van.

Our family camper mainly had personal items in it: boxes of books and kitchenware, black bin liners full of clothes, lots of spare bedding. Mum, Flick and the boys got to work hefting it out and trotting to and from the farmhouse with load after load.

The back of Nuncle's van, though, was an Aladdin's cave. Too small to carry anything, I watched as he and Dad got to work unloading boxes of tools, bits of machinery, all sorts of stuff. As each item was hauled to the front of the van and wrestled onto the ground I'd ask, "What's that?" It became a game, with Nuncle and Dad both happy to go into detail about what each thing was, most of which went straight over my head.

I recognised the shape of Nuncle's guitar in its case and was pleased it made the journey. He always got it out at family get-togethers and made us join in with a singalong, whether we liked it or not. Then a large chest freezer was inched forward and Nuncle explained, "Once this is up and running we can freeze food for the winter."

"What?" I asked. "Like frozen chips?"

They both laughed.

"Not quite, Alice," said Dad. "We fatten up the pigs during the summer and have them butchered to give us meat for the winter."

So the little piglets were going to die? Nuncle saw my bottom lip tremble. He squatted down in front of me and gave me a cuddle. "Oh, munchkin, don't be sad. It's where all the sausages and bacon you like come from."

Dad was more matter-of-fact. "That's life on a farm, Alice. Better get used to it."

After that, I stood out of the way while they finished unloading. The camper was soon empty and Mum, Flick and my brothers went inside to start preparing lunch. I waited while the last few bits and pieces were hauled from the depths of the rusty transit. Dad and Nuncle looked satisfied. "Off you go inside now, Alice. Check on lunch."

"Aren't you coming?"

"Not just yet."

I headed in but, turning, saw them kneeling down on the bare boards of the empty van. Dad took a screwdriver and started to work at one of the floorboards. When the board was loose, Nuncle lifted it to one side while Dad reached and took out a tightly wrapped parcel, a few feet long, thick at one end, tapering down at the other.

Dad unwrapped it while Nuncle leaned deeper into the hiding place and brought up a succession of small, neat boxes. In a few seconds Dad had the parcel unwrapped.

A shotgun.

He examined it carefully, cracked open the stock, stared down the barrels, then clicked it shut again and held it up to his shoulder.

I backed out of sight.

Then turned and ran inside.

9

That first summer has a golden halo.

I know it couldn't have been as nice as I remember but that's the problem with memories.

The bad times make the good ones feel better than they were.

Or maybe it's the good things that make the bad things bearable.

Either way, you have to hold on to the good memories or the bad ones will overwhelm you.

Hold on to them.

Tight.

Scotland is meant to be cold and wet but that summer the weather was wonderful. Warm and sunny day followed warm and sunny day. Tom, Rich and I couldn't believe our luck. Even doing chores like feeding the pigs or collecting eggs was new and exciting and barely felt like work.

When we weren't helping on the farm or having lessons with Flick, we could come and go as we pleased. Running through the fields. Splashing in the stream. Climbing trees in the woods behind the farmhouse. There were no busy roads, no traffic to look out for, no supervised visits to the local park. We had the run of the place.

By the end of June we didn't even have lessons to bother us. Tom and Rich pointed out that this should have been our school summer holidays and so home school was officially shut down until September.

Flick, too, was glad of the rest. The bump of her tummy was getting bigger by the day and I understood what Nuncle meant by 'unexpected guests'. I'd put a tentative hand on the bump a few times, withdrawing as if scalded if I felt some movement inside.

"Don't be frightened, it's only a baby," she said.

Only.

In the orchard we made a rope swing and my brothers, urged on by me, would try to make it loop-the-loop. "Higher! Higher!" I'd shout, giggling so hard I could barely get my breath, but they could never quite manage it. It stayed light so late that we'd play out again after supper, drinking in the twilight, lying on our backs in the grass as dancing clouds of midges formed over the tops of the trees. We'd watch the colours of sunset retreat as the night sky awakened, each of us straining to be the first to spot an emerging star.

"It's not so bad here, is it," said Rich one particularly perfect evening.

Tom got him in a headlock and they started a wrestling match. In our old life, I might have called Mum. Instead, I piled in on top and added a few grapples and punches of my own to the melee.

We'd stay outside until Mum called us to bed and then a little longer. By the time we went in it would be all I could do to keep my eyes open. I'd try to describe my day to her as she helped me undress, some new detail of nature I'd noticed, something funny one of the boys had said or done. Often I'd be asleep before she'd even closed my bedroom door.

One night, Nuncle came and shook me awake. I woke with

a start to see him bending over me. Rich and Tom lurked in the doorway, yawning. "Hey, munchkin, want to come stargazing with us?"

I wasn't actually sure that I did. It was very warm and cosy in my bed.

"There's a big meteor shower. We might see shooting stars," Nuncle explained. Now this did seem like a good reason to get up. And, from the tiptoeing and whispering, I understood that my parents didn't know we were up. Which gave the whole thing an added air of excitement.

We crept downstairs and put on our coats. Even if it was summer, Scottish nights are chilly. Outside, Nuncle was carrying a couple of large blankets. He lay one down on a patch of grass and we all lay on it. Then he pulled the other one up over us. "Like sardines," he said.

The Milky Way arched over our heads. Around it, countless stars, more and more the longer we looked.

"There's one!" said Tom excitedly. A finger flew up from under the blanket as a white trail burst across the sky. He was pleased to be the first of us to see anything.

"Well done, Tom," said Nuncle. "Now, everyone keep your eyes peeled. Let's see how many we can count."

"How many stars are there?" I asked.

"Oh, millions and millions," said Nuncle.

"And do they all have people on them?"

The boys mocked me for this. "Don't be silly, their feet would get very hot."

Nuncle was, typically, all patience. "All the stars are suns, like our Sun. So they're too hot for anyone to live on. But lots of them have planets going around them, just like our Sun does. And some of them might well have people living on them."

"People like us?"

"Maybe. Or they could look very different to us. We don't know."

"Do you think their planets are better than ours?"

"Leave it out with the questions," said Rich. "This is meant to be fun not a science lesson."

"She's just interested, Rich," said Nuncle. "Well, I certainly hope so, munchkin" he said. "You'd have to think there's someone smarter than us in the universe."

Nuncle told us the names of some of the bright summer stars and we counted shooting stars until, only a couple of hours later, dawn began to break.

And that's how Mum found us at breakfast time, when she got tired of shouting upstairs and came looking outside. Four of us dozing under a blanket on the grass, "Like a litter of piglets. And making a similar noise, too."

10

At summer's end the local village held its annual fete. By then we'd been regular enough at church for Dad to be less concerned about awkward questions and he agreed that we could go. "It will be good to mix with some of the locals."

"Do you think you're up to it, Flick?" asked Mum.

"If the alternative is spending Saturday night stuck here while you all have fun, I'm up to it."

"Don't worry, I'll keep her off the cider," said Nuncle.

The hour-long walk into the village didn't seem nearly as long with the promise of cola, cakes and fireworks at the other end of it. Flick's progress was slow and she stopped for rests now and then. Nuncle hung back with her and I tagged along with them while my parents and the boys disappeared from view up ahead. I had another tentative feel of the bump.

"Do you know if it's a boy or a girl?" I asked.

"Not yet."

"We want it to be a surprise," Nuncle explained.

"Mum said that, before she had me, she went to the hospital and there was a special machine that told her I was a girl. And she was really happy because she had two boys already and didn't want another one."

"I don't blame her," said Flick.

"Yes, they could do that at hospitals. It was called a scan. But we've not had one of those have we?"

Flick shook her head. "Women were having babies for thousands of years without hospitals and scans. We're going to have our baby at home. You can help if you like?"

I nodded, although I wasn't entirely sure that I wanted to help. It was one thing to touch the bump or hold a baby, another thing entirely to see one arrive. "I'd like it to be a girl so that I have someone to play with when the boys are too old to play with me."

Flick had to stop again, bending at the waist with her hands on her knees.

"Are you okay, love?" asked Nuncle.

She winced and rubbed her swollen tummy.

"I don't think you should go, love," he said. "The walk's too much for you."

Flick straightened up, took a deep breath and blew it out again.

"It's passed, I'm okay."

"Don't be daft. You're pushing yourself too hard. Let's go back."

"This might be the last chance we get to let our hair down."

"Sod that. We can let our hair down after the baby's born. Alice, will you be okay to catch up with the others by yourself?"

It was still broad daylight and I knew the way. "Of course I will."

"Off you go then. We'll watch 'til you're out of sight. Tell your mum and dad that Flick's tired and we're going back to the farm."

"Okay, hope you feel better, Flick."

"Thanks, love."

I set off at a trot. Before I disappeared from view I turned around to give them a wave. They waved back and I carried on running along the rutted path. A little further up ahead I could see Mum and Dad and slowed down to a walk, reassured at having them in sight.

"Boo!"

My heart leaped as a figure jumped from the bushes onto the path in front of me. Without thinking, head down, teeth gritted, I kicked out as hard as I could at my attacker. The toe of my shoe connected and I looked up as Rich doubled-over in agony and collapsed in a heap. He lay down on one side in front of me, slowly drew his knees up toward his chin, and cupped himself between his legs. All the while emitting a low groan.

Tom emerged from the undergrowth and looked down at our stricken brother. "I told you not to do it," he said, devoid of sympathy, before bellowing, "Mum, Alice has kicked Rich's balls in!"

Up ahead my parents stopped, turned around, and slowly trudged back the way they'd come.

"Can't we leave you alone for ten minutes?" said Dad, looking fiercely at each of us in turn. "This was meant to be a treat."

Mum was helping Rich back into a sitting position. I could feel myself getting upset. All I'd done was defend myself. "But he jumped out at me," I explained as my eyes started to sting.

"Tom, what happened?" asked Mum.

"Rich thought it would be brilliant to scare Alice. We hid in the bushes and he jumped out as she went past. So she kicked him in the nuts." Before adding, after a pause for emphasis, "Really hard."

Mum looked down at the ground, trying to suppress a smile. Then I knew that I wasn't in trouble and began to feel better.

"Now, Alice, you can't go around kicking your brothers in the... nuts," Dad said, looking me straight in the eye. "But, if you're ever on your own, and someone jumps out and scares you, you kick them right where you kicked Rich as hard as you possibly can. Okay?"

"Okay."

Mum helped him back to his feet. "Where's Nick and Flick?" she asked me.

"Flick wasn't very well. Nuncle said we should go without them."

"Adam, isn't it time she saw a doctor?" asked Mum.

"Haven't we covered this? They knew when we left. They were completely fine with it then. Flick was all about the home birth, doing it naturally, all that."

"But what if there's a problem?"

"She was just tired. Isn't that right, Alice?" Dad looked over at me for confirmation. I wasn't sure but I nodded anyway.

"You were tired all the time with these three. But there weren't any problems… at the births, I mean."

Mum stood, looking down, concern etched across her face.

"Rest, that's all she needs. Now, are we going to the village or aren't we?"

He put his arm around Mum's shoulders and, reluctantly at first, she started down the path again. The three of us fell in step behind.

It was the first time I'd ever been to a village fete. And, as it turned out, the last.

It was great fun at first. The fallow field next to the church was laid out with trestle tables and dressed in bunting. There was a band and a raffle and girls in kilts dancing. There were sheep and pigs in pens and prize cows were given awards. There was cake and crisps and cloudy lemonade so sour it made my teeth tingle. Mum and Dad spoke to lots of different people and they all seemed very nice. She introduced me to an old lady with friendly eyes.

"What did you think of your first Scottish summer?" the lady asked.

I said that I liked it very much.

"Ah, but we'll pay for it this winter," she said. "Just you wait and see."

She left me with her granddaughter, a girl I recognised from church who looked my age. "Hello, I'm Alice. What's your name?"

"I'm Maggie. Is that your mum?"

I nodded.

"She's very pretty."

"Thanks. Where's your mum?"

"She's in the army. So was my dad but he got killed. I live with my nan now."

Children have no words at moments like this but adults really aren't much better. We said goodbye and drifted off from one another.

The fireworks that marked the end of the day lit up the sky after sunset. I couldn't help thinking they weren't as beautiful as the stars they were obscuring. People started to head off home. As me and my brothers made our way to where our parents stood chatting, an older boy approached us.

"My dad says you're English?"

We nodded.

"My dad says the English are wankers."

I didn't know what that word meant but I could tell by my brothers' faces that it wasn't very nice. I thought about kicking him where I'd kicked Rich but had done enough nut-kicking for one day. The boy was a couple of inches taller than Tom and a full head taller than Rich. But that didn't stop him. Rich leapt at the older boy, grabbed him around the neck with one arm and started pummelling him in the face with the other.

Immediately, there was a crowd around us. Adults came and pulled the two boys apart, the local boy's nose all bloodied, Rich's face red with rage and exertion.

"What the bloody Hell…?" Dad pushed his way through the crowd, grabbed Rich by the shoulders and shook him. "Did you hit this boy? Did you hit this boy?" Rich started to snivel. This enraged Dad even more. He struck him across the face with the flat of his hand.

"Adam!" yelled Mum.

It was the first time Dad had hit any of us. Rich, stunned, stopped snivelling and just stood there, frozen, with his mouth hanging open.

That was that. We walked home in silence following the bobbing beam of my dad's torch. Tom tried to get Rich's attention a couple of times but he wasn't interested. He trudged on, head down, hands deep in his pockets.

The walk seemed much longer this time but the farm drew gradually nearer. In the distance a light was burning from Nick and Flick's bedroom window, cutting through the treacly darkness. We took the path across the field and skirted the vegetable patch, Dad's torch beam dancing across the rutted surfaces, glancing onto the creamy stone walls.

The kitchen door was open but no light came from inside.

Then we saw Nuncle. Slumped on the doorstep, eyes closed, his head resting on the wooden frame. The torchlight seemed to drain all colour from his face so that he looked like a waxwork. His wrists were resting on his knees and his hands hung limply from them.

They were covered in blood.

Dad gave Rich the flashlight, strode up to the doorway and shook Nuncle by the shoulder. "Nick. Nick. Are you okay?"

Nuncle didn't move but he slowly opened his eyes and looked up at Dad. It was as if he were looking at a complete stranger.

Mum knelt down beside him, took his head in her hands and turned it to look into his eyes. "Nick, what's happened? Is this your blood?"

He dredged up the answer. "Not my blood. Flick's."

Mum stared past him, into the darkness of the farmhouse. Still cradling Nuncle's hand, she turned and looked at Dad, sternly imploring. He got the message.

"Kids, stay here."

He stepped past her, over the threshold, into the darkness of the kitchen. The boys were silent, Tom holding the beam of the torch on Nick and Mum. I edged towards the door and wrapped my hand around one of Nuncle's bloodied fingers.

"Nuncle, Rich hit a boy. At the fair."

He looked at me with no recognition. I felt it like a physical shock. I'd always been Nuncle's favourite, the centre of attention whenever he was present, but whatever had happened to Flick had so shaken him that he didn't even know me.

I let go of the finger and took a step back.

On an impulse, I ducked past them and dove into the house. Maybe if I could help Flick, or find out what was wrong with her, Nuncle would feel better and like me again.

Mum shouted, "Alice, come back!" but she didn't leave Nuncle, didn't follow me in.

I ran through the kitchen, into the hall, up the stairs. The light from their bedroom spilled out across the landing through the half-open door. I grabbed the knob and pushed the door all the way open.

Bloodied sheets and towels were heaped on the floor. White linens soaked in red. It was close in the room and a hot, iron stink clung to the air. The mattress, too, was soaked in blood. It had been stripped of its sheets and Flick lay on it, her thin nightie glued to her and rendered almost transparent with sweat. Beneath it her tummy, which I'd watch swell month by month, seen move of its own accord as new life kicked inside it, was flat.

Dad was on his hands and knees at the foot of the bed, mopping up blood with more towels. Flick lay on her side facing the door. Her face, like Nuncle's, was ashen. Her half-open eyes were blank with despair. She saw me in the doorway and a thin, bitter smile stretched across her lips.

"No little sister for you, Alice," she croaked.

On the floor was a washing up bowl, partly filled with water. At the bottom, curled up small, cruelly still, was a tiny, purple, wrinkled body. Smaller than one of my dolls. A fleshy tube ran from its tummy to a red, veiny lump. The whole mess glistened.

Hearing Flick's voice, Dad's head snapped up. He dropped the towels, leapt to his feet and strode over towards me, his face a mask.

I quickly stepped backwards, out of the room.

He slammed the door shut in my face.

11

The next morning, Dad and Nuncle were arguing when I came down for breakfast.

I stood in the kitchen doorway, silent and unobserved, as they fought about the baby and what should be done with the remains. Nuncle wanted her buried in the church cemetery. Dad argued this would create more awkward questions, more potential for involvement with the authorities.

"Why don't we just flush her down the toilet then? Or, better still, feed her to the pigs."

I'd not heard that kind of bitterness from Nuncle before and it frightened me.

But Dad was cold and unfeeling, which frightened me even more. "Don't be childish, Nick. That's not what I'm saying and you know it. If you want her buried at the church they'll need a death certificate. To get one of those, you have to take her body to the hospital. They might even want to do an autopsy. Do you want to go through all that? Do you want to put Flick through all of that?" He sat down and put an arm around him. "We can bury her here," said Dad, softening, "find a piece of ground on the farm. Then Flick can visit as often as she likes, keep it nice, plant flowers."

"If we'd gone to hospital in the first place we would never have lost her."

"You don't know that's true so don't try to park it on me. You both said you wanted a home birth."

Dad looked around and saw me hovering.

"You again?"

I felt ashamed. As if, for the second time in quick succession, I'd intruded on some dreadful adult business that I shouldn't have witnessed.

"Go outside and play with your brothers." His voice had a harsh, authoritative tone.

I didn't dare ask about breakfast.

Tom and Rich were down by the stream. They weren't doing much, just silently watching the water. I flopped down next to them on the shallow bank.

"You too?" said Tom.

I nodded.

I sat with my knees tucked under my chin, arms folded tightly around them. I put my head down and started to cry.

"Hungry?" asked Rich.

I looked up and nodded. He dug an apple out of his pocket and passed it to me. I took a big bite and started to feel better.

"Do you think we'll go back home now?" Rich asked.

"Of course not," answered Tom. "You heard what Dad said. This is our home. Better get used to it."

There was an awkward silence, eventually broken by Rich. "Alice, what did it look like?"

Tom gave him a filthy look. "You don't have to tell him anything, Alice. He's sick."

"Spoilsport," said Rich. "I was only curious."

"It's funny but Flick said the baby would be my sister," I told them.

"She meant cousin," said Rich.

"I know that but what she said was 'sister'."

"She'd lost about a gallon of blood, Alice. And she was exhausted. She could have said anything," Tom explained.

In the end, Nuncle allowed Flick to decide where to bury the baby. She was beyond caring and so took the route of least resistance. Another triumph for Dad's powers of persuasion.

So, the following day, we all gathered in the orchard. Nick carried Flick outside, wrapped in a large blanket, and placed her on one of the kitchen chairs. He stood beside her throughout, a supportive arm around her, while Mum stood on the other side casting anxious sideways glances at them both.

The boys had been told to dig a deep hole at the base of the tallest, strongest apple tree, deep so that foxes wouldn't disturb her, and this was where she was placed, wrapped in a small, bright pink blanket that I didn't use any more.

Dad did a reading from the Bible and then Tom and Rich filled in the hole, taking handfuls of loose soil and carefully lowering each one into the tiny grave. It was as if they didn't want to injure the poor thing, but what harm could come to her now? I watched the black earth consume the pink of the blanket. Soon, baby and shroud were hidden from view, the ritual complete. Tom gently patted the soil down and Nuncle put a smooth, flat stone he'd found by the stream on top and pushed it into the soft earth.

We were a sombre group but no one cried.

Not even Flick. Who was lost somewhere deep inside herself.

12

The following day we had a visitor.

People had been to the farm before, of course. Farmers with deliveries of chickens, piglets and feed. Local tradesmen with building materials. The vicar when he came to greet the district's new family. But Dad always knew in advance that those people were coming.

This visitor was a surprise.

Tom and Rich had been working in the field with Nuncle when they came sprinting into the kitchen. "There's a policeman coming," panted Tom. Mum and I had been making a cake for Flick, who was still very weak. Mum wiped her hands and went to fetch Dad, leaving us to stare wide-eyed at one another.

"Do you think it's cos you hit that boy, Rich?" I asked.

It was what all three of us were thinking.

"I barely touched him," he said.

"What if he's dead?" I wondered out loud.

"He might have had a haemorrhage or something," said Tom, adding fuel to the fire.

Nuncle came in with the policeman. They were talking in a friendly way, which put me more at ease.

A moment later, Mum came in with Dad.

The policeman was very smiley, introduced himself as PC Smith and shook everyone's hand, including mine.

"So who's this little lady?" he asked me.

"I'm Alice."

"Nice to meet you, Alice," he said as he sat down, took off his hat and unbuttoned his coat. He was older than my parents, perhaps in his fifties, which seemed ancient to me. He was a little overweight too but that wasn't yet a rarity. "What's a man got to do to get a cup of tea around here?"

Mum laughed. "Of course. Tea all round? Alice, you'll help me won't you."

I joined her at the sink, rinsing out mugs and putting tea bags into them.

Dad sat down with Nuncle and PC Smith. "So, what can we do for you, Officer?"

"Ah, I'm just the local bobby, there's no need to call me 'officer'. You can call me Brian."

"That's nice of you, Officer, but what can we do for you?"

The policeman remained relaxed and informal despite Dad's hostility.

"I thought I should come up here and introduce myself. You people are part of the community now, and we're all about community around here."

Rich nervously piped up. "Is... is that boy okay?"

PC Smith laughed. "Oh, laddie, there's nothing to worry about on that score. Davey Hyde's a tearaway like his father. From what I hear, he had it coming. There's no excuse for foul language in front of lady. However young she is." He ruffled Rich's hair. "You gave that big lad a pasting right enough," he said, before adding, more pointedly, to my dad, "we may have need for fighters before long."

"If you're not here to arrest my ten-year-old son, what are you here for?"

"I wonder if this conversation might better be had without the wee ones present?"

Dad disagreed. "We're a family. We've been through enough together already. They can stay."

"In which case, I wondered if you could confirm the full name of everyone who lives in the property." PC Smith, all business now, took out his notebook and pencil and began writing things down.

"Of course. I'm Alan Rogers, this is my brother Duncan and my wife Judy." I didn't know why my dad was giving false names but I knew enough to keep quiet. "And these are our children: Tom, Rich and Alice."

"I believe there's a seventh person who lives with you?"

"That's my wife Gayle," said Nuncle.

"She's the pregnant lady, I understand?"

"Not anymore. We... we lost the baby, I'm afraid."

"Oh, I'm sorry to hear that, truly sorry. It all tallies with what I've heard in the village. Only one thing confuses me."

"Which is?" asked Dad.

"Why, at the fair last weekend, your wife referred to you as 'Adam'?"

Mum dropped the mug she was washing. It made a harsh, clattering sound in the sink. I looked over in time to see her recompose herself. Dad, too, was thinking on his feet, eager not to betray any anxiety.

"Are you sure?" he said with mock casualness.

"Oh, I'm sure right enough. I asked half a dozen people and they all heard her say the same thing. Your wife," he checked his notes, "Judy, shouted the name 'Adam' at you when you were disciplining young Rich here. I heard it with my own ears, too. We don't have the village fete but once a year so, when we do, I don't like to miss out on the occasion."

A painful silence. It only lasted a few seconds but it felt a lot longer.

"A slip of the tongue, I'm sure," ventured Dad.

"Perhaps, perhaps. My wife calls me all sorts of things not to be repeated in polite company. But even she doesn't get my Christian name wrong."

The whistling kettle broke the tension. Mum and I handed the cups of tea round.

"Thanks ever so much, Mrs Rogers," said PC Smith. He blew on his tea and took a sip, eyeing my dad over the top of the mug as he did so. Then he placed the mug down carefully on the kitchen table.

"I don't suppose I could trouble you for some identification?"

"Of course." Dad stood up from the table and left the room. We heard his feet retreat down the hallway.

In his absence, none of us spoke or even sipped our tea. Except for PC Smith who took long, loud slurps from his. He looked around the kitchen. "I like what you've done with the place. It needed sprucing up. Old Jack Bridges hadn't given it a lick of paint in decades."

My father's footsteps could be heard returning down the corridor. He strode into the kitchen carrying, not passports, but a shotgun. He planted his feet firmly and levelled the weapon at PC Smith's face. "Both barrels are loaded," he said.

Mum screamed. "Adam! What are you doing? Have you lost your mind?"

Nuncle stood up from the table as if stung. He backed away against the wall and motioned for the boys and me to do the same. We edged towards him, not taking our eyes off the scene unfolding at the table.

Smith, though, remained calm. "Ah, so it is Adam, then?"

"What do you want?" my father asked him. "Money?"

"I thought you were going to say 'I'm not afraid to use this' or some such nonsense. I've been staring down the barrels of angry farmers' shotguns for thirty years and I've never once seen a man use it with his entire family in the same room. Lead shot is no great respecter of wives and children, and certainly not designed for indoor use."

Mum was on the verge of hysteria. "For God's sake, Adam."

"Bloody hell, Adam, you're not going to shoot a policeman, they'll throw the book at us," Nuncle entreated.

"Then answer the goddam question."

Smith continued, still calm. "I came here to clear up a little mystery, that's all. People come to my district to live peaceably, I have no axe to grind. It is, of course, an offence to give false information to officials or to possess fraudulent identification documents. Those are the sorts of offences that, in these troubled times, carry severe penalties."

Dad brought the barrels of the shotgun within inches of Smith's face.

"So what do you intend to do about it?"

For the first time Smith's voice betrayed mounting tension. "Those things have been known to go off by accident, you know."

Dad didn't move the shotgun away. Not even an inch.

"I'm just a bobby, making first contact," Smith continued. "I'm here to let you know that there are many who sympathise with a young family looking for a safe haven. You contribute fully to village life, you'll be fine here, no questions asked."

"How do I know I can trust you?"

"Because if you couldn't, why would I come here alone? Unarmed? Hell, the walk from the village is a ball ache at the best of times." Smith was calm again now. "If you couldn't trust me, there'd be an armoured column outside and men with a lot more firepower than that," he nodded his head towards the shotgun inches from his nose, "at their disposal."

Dad slowly lowered the gun. Smith drew a breath. Then picked up his tea and started to slurp it again. Dad sat down opposite him and rested the butt of the shogun on the floor.

"Perhaps you're right. This is a conversation we should have without the kids present."

Nuncle motioned with his head for us all to leave and, without needing to be told twice, we rushed outside.

"Did you see Dad with that shotgun? How cool was that," said Rich once we were a comfortable distance from the house.

"It wouldn't have been so cool if it had gone off. If he'd killed the copper, he'd be executed," reasoned Tom.

"Only if they found out. We could bury him in the orchard, like Flick's baby."

Rich was only ten months younger than Tom, but sometimes even I felt older than him.

After an hour or so outside, with twilight gathering, we saw Mum, Dad and Nuncle at the kitchen door. They all shook hands with Smith then Dad lead him down through the garden to the edge of our property. They shook hands again and we watched as he disappeared down the rutted path and was consumed by the gloom.

Dad strode back to the farmhouse, yelling to us, "You three, supper." We climbed down from the wall and followed him into the house.

13

It was autumn now and I'd become easy with the highland mornings and the farmhouse routine that started each day.

I'd wake to the clattering of pans in the kitchen below my bedroom. Water chugging from the tap into my mum's tin kettle, the kettle clanging into place on the burner of the wood-fired stove and then, a few minutes later, the whistle of boiling water.

That whistle was my alarm clock.

I'd climb out of bed and sneak a look out of the window, taking in the view across the kitchen garden, the lower field, the stream and woods beyond. Sometimes, when the weather closed in, I couldn't see further than the garden for a fine mist of drizzle. But on clear mornings I could see all the way to the mountains.

Those were the mornings that I loved.

I'd dash down the stairs, pull on my wellies and coat, and then present myself to Mum. She'd bend down, zip up my anorak, and give me a bucket of kitchen scraps and peelings.

"Breakfast in ten minutes," she'd say, opening the back door for me.

Then I'd be off outside, the clean air hitting me like cold water, my boots leaving tiny footprints in the dewy morning grass.

First stop, the pigsty. The remaining pigs, the ones that hadn't been sold off or butchered for our winter meat supply, would come snuffling and snorting towards me, their bodies steaming. I'd empty the kitchen scraps into the feeder and watch as they buried their hot snouts into them, greedily gobbling them up.

Bucket empty, my next stop was the orchard to collect windfall apples.

The night before *that* morning had been quite windy, so I expected a good haul. I blew breath clouds on the way to the orchard, alternating between blowing out through my nose and then my mouth, taking big lungfuls of air that puffed out my chest, and blowing them out like steam from the kettle, making the most of the morning chill.

It made me think of the enormous clouds given off by the cows I'd seen driven to milking in the narrow lanes around our farm. I played at being a cow, lurching from side to side, picking up my feet and stomping them down in the wet grass, even emitting a few deep, resonant 'moos'.

I turned the corner, through the old stone arch that lead into the orchard. I was right. The wind had dislodged a record number of apples, even in this sheltered spot. I began moving through the orchard, bending down to pick up the damp apples and placing them carefully in the bucket so as not to bruise them.

I moved deeper into the orchard, getting into a nice rhythm. Bend, pick, place, move, bend, pick, place, move, my eyes scanning the ground for the next nearest pick. The bucket was getting heavier now. I put it down and stood up to stretch out my back.

That's when I saw her.

Feet swaying gently in the air a few feet in front of me.

A kitchen chair on its side in the grass.

My eyes travelled up from her feet, moved slowly up her naked legs and across the dark stain on the groin of her nightdress. The struggle between life and death had forced her to empty herself. On, inexorably, unable to look away, my eyes travelled up her torso, took in the limply swaying arms, and then locked onto the rope around her neck. It had dug into the flesh as it took her weight and pushed it up under her chin like a collar. The rope had dug into her so tight even my small hands would have been able to form a complete circle around her neck.

And on, inevitably, to her face.

It was an even deeper purple than the blood she had shed trying to bring a life into the world.

Her tongue stuck out at an obscene angle.

Her lifeless eyes bulged grotesquely.

She had chosen a strong branch above the spot where her baby's tiny body had been placed. I don't know how long I stood there, taking in the awfulness of Flick's gently swaying corpse. But then I turned and ran, sprinted back to the house, upsetting the bucket of apples as I fled.

I couldn't speak. I stood in the kitchen, panting for breath, staring at Mum's back while she busied herself preparing breakfast.

"Did you find apples?"

She turned and saw me and knew without asking that something was terribly, terribly wrong.

Then my bladder betrayed me and I peed all over the tiled floor.

14

Mum tried to get me to speak but couldn't.

This scared her more than anything so she got Dad.

He retraced my steps around the farm and soon found Flick. He cut her down, laid her out on the grass, put a sheet over her. Then he went to find his brother and break the news.

The news broke Nuncle.

He raged against our decision to leave our homes in England.

He raged against the loss of his wife and baby daughter.

He raged against my dad for causing all this.

He exploded when Flick's funeral was discussed. Not that anyone, even Dad, suggested that a hole in the orchard was a suitable resting place.

For many nights afterwards, I couldn't sleep.

Mum stayed with me, curled up in my little bed, her arms wrapped around me. She slept, but I did not. Her being there did, though, keep the Scarecrow away.

In the house, everything was broken.

Mum fought with Dad.

Dad fought with Nuncle. Really fought, not just with words.

Tom and Rich looked on silently until, glutted on misery, they went outside and stayed there, dawn to dusk, for days on end. If it had been summer, I don't think they would have come home at all. But the cold nights always forced them back indoors eventually.

I didn't row with anyone, didn't speak to anyone, not even to Nuncle when he sobbed and begged me to tell him how I'd found her. The words weren't there. Afterwards, he'd hug me and say sorry over and over for pressing me but his hugs had lost their power to heal.

Everything Dad had wanted to avoid – police, hospitals, the authorities and, as a consequence, discovery – looked inevitable now. But Smith proved a friend to us and persuaded the village doctor to falsify Flick's death certificate. While the vicar turned a blind eye to the church's traditional ban on burying suicides.

It was a small ceremony, only the six of us and Rev. Haigh. I don't remember anyone making a single sound. Even Nuncle had cried out all his tears. He stayed behind long after we left to make the long march back to the farm.

"Why did Flick do it?" asked Rich to break the agonising silence.

"She wasn't strong enough," Dad answered.

The next morning I was woken by the sound of an engine turning over, leapt out of bed and looked out of the window. It was barely light. Mum was still spending the nights in my room and joined me at the window. Together, we peered outside.

Below us, the removal van was reversing out of the barn, white headlights cutting through the dark. It swung around in front of the house.

Nuncle was driving it.

Of course.

Mum gasped and ran out of the room.

I watched from the window as she appeared outside, ghostlike in her white nightie. She ran to the driver's side and grabbed the handle, tried to pull open the door but it was locked. She hammered at the window with her fists, her voice cutting through the morning stillness, "Nick! Nick! Please don't leave me."

He drove on.

Mum was spun around by the van and sank to her knees in the dirt of the vegetable garden. She bowed her head and sobbed. Giving no thought to the cold, I went outside barefoot and joined her. She was still kneeling in the dirt, wracking sobs coming from a place deep inside her. I watched the lights of the removal van disappear into the distance and only then did I look back towards the house.

Dad was framed in the doorway, watching impassively, arms folded across his chest. He didn't come out and join us. When he knew that I'd seen him he went back inside.

It was a few minutes before Mum clawed herself up out of the mud. Her face was a mess of tears and snot.

"I'd better start breakfast," she said.

She ran the sleeve of her nightie across her face, brushed the mud from her knees, and headed back to the house. I trudged along behind her.

After that, winter came.

And it was bitter.

PART II

1

Eyes. Throat. Groin.

That's what Argyll taught me.

These are the most vulnerable parts of a man's body. (And your attacker is more likely to be a man than a woman.)

Go for the eyes first because you can kill him if you get it right. And a pointy stick, a pencil, even a finger can be enough to do the job. Then the throat. Jab the windpipe with anything sharp. Use your elbow or the side of your hand and karate chop him across it. Or get both hands around his throat and squeeze. Hard.

Of course, both of these defences mean you've been attacked from the front. If he grabs you from behind, kick your legs backwards into his groin. He'll go down like a sack of spuds. (I knew this was true from the time I kicked Rich on the way to the church fete… many years ago now.) But it only takes a few minutes for them to recover so, while he's down, stick a blade in him. Or, if there's no time and your courage fails you, *run*. Fast.

Eyes. Throat. Groin.

Remember it. Like a song in your head.

Eyes. Throat. Groin.

Eyes. Throat. Groin.

2

It was the dogs that woke us.

Which, after all, was the whole point of having them.

Dad had warned me against getting too attached when he first brought them home. "They're not pets," he'd said as I fussed over them. "And they're not to live in the house. They're border collies, the cleverest breed of dog there is. You can train them to do all sorts of things. Around here, they're used as sheepdogs mainly but they're going to be our guard dogs."

I didn't care what they were or why Dad had got them. I just loved them.

He brought them that first spring, around the anniversary of our arrival, an attempt to cheer us after our first grim winter. I held one in either hand, bringing them up to my face in turn, kissing their noses.

"Come on, kids, what would you like to call them?" Dad asked, trying to turn the naming into a bonding family moment. "One's a girl, one's a boy. We can all put names into a hat and pull them out."

Mum hung back, arms folded across her chest.

"Why don't we call them Nick and Flick?" Tom suggested dryly. Rich snorted his approval.

Instantly, Dad's attitude switched. The smile was put

away and the stern, frowning figure that we'd known since the previous winter, when his grand plan had seemed to disintegrate, was back in control. It was as if he had a button in his head that he could flick. Maybe he'd toyed with the idea of being the dad we remembered from St Albans again. Maybe. But Tom's sarcastic outburst put a stop to that and he didn't try to reach out to us again.

"If that's how you want it." He tried to take the puppies back from me but I wouldn't let go. They whimpered as we performed a tug of war over them.

"No, Dad, no. Let me name them. Please."

My pleading had the desired effect.

"Okay, but if you don't have anything by the morning, I'm going to call them 'Dog' and 'Bitch' and that will be the end of it."

I lay awake all night, different names tumbling over in my mind. In the end, I decided we'd call the boy pup Blackie, as his coat was mainly black with some white patches and the girl would be Violet, after my best friend from school.

Back when I used to go to school.

Back when I had a best friend.

I had no friends here and I missed them. My brothers were good to play with, especially as I could be as rough with them as I wanted and they weren't allowed to be as rough back. But friends my own age would have been nice.

Especially a girl.

I suppose, in a childish way, I hoped that my new dog Violet would make up for it. That had been four years earlier. By now, Blackie and Vi were full grown and Dad, despite being adamant that they weren't family pets, was glad that I'd bonded with them early.

They kept me company on my walks to the village or when I went into the woods to collect mushrooms or berries or check the snares. Never more than a couple of feet away from me. Sniffing the air. Growling. Alert to danger. Occasionally they'd catch the scent of something wild and tear off into the undergrowth after it. But they always returned to heel when I called them.

At night they slept outside in kennels Tom and Rich had built for them. In winter they shared one kennel and one another's warmth. They'd already proved themselves useful on dozens of occasions, sniffing out poachers and prowlers who always received the same warm welcome: angry teeth, sharp claws and my dad's shotgun levelled at their faces.

Blackie and Vi could smell trouble on the wind and would bark their lungs out to alert us to it.

That was the case this time too.

Their barks seeped into my dream and, after a few moments, drew me up from the depths of it. I shot out of bed, darted across the room to the window and flung back the curtains.

There was already a commotion outside.

The beam of Dad's torchlight bobbed as he dashed around the side of the house to the barn. Moments after Dad had gone from sight, the dogs appeared, two swift arrows sprinting across the potato field towards the stream.

A moment later still, the whirr of the generator as the floodlights that marked out our perimeter were switched on. Then Dad reappeared, accompanied by Argyll, both of them carrying shotguns. They jog-trotted after the dogs.

Quickly, I drew on my boots, threw a jumper on over my nightie and dashed from the room.

"What's going on?" Tom asked, yawning in his bedroom doorway as I sped past him.

"I don't know but I'm going to find out."

I clomped down the stairs, grabbed my coat from the hook on the back of the kitchen door and ran outside, shoving my arms into the sleeves as I went. My torch lived in one deep pocket and I pulled it loose and switched it on. It helped me see the way, of course, and also made me less likely to surprise Dad and Argyll; I was eager to be part of the action but not so keen to get a face full of lead shot.

I raced across the field, the dancing beam of my torch lighting the way, warning me of furrows, roots, rocks. My warm breath trailed a cloud of steam after me in the icy night air.

(I'm pretty certain it was February but I could be wrong. The jumper I'd pulled on was a gift from Mum the previous Christmas – her knitting skills had come on in leaps and bounds over the years – and, given I hadn't already reduced it to ribbons, it must have been early in the year.)

Panting, I scrambled down, up and over the ditch and stone wall that protected the far end of the field. I leapt onto the path the other side and ran on towards where my dad's torch was fixed on an area of reeds and undergrowth on the far side of the stream.

The dogs were splashing about in the shallows, kicking up water and getting in Dad's light. It was his turn to bark. "Blackie! Vi! For Christ's sake, get out of the way."

I felt a dry branch give under my foot, heard it crack and was instantly blinded by the beam of Dad's torch.

"Who the Hell is that?"

I stopped running and put one hand across my eyes, shielding them from the stinging light. "It's me, Dad."

"What are you doing out of bed?"

"I heard the dogs."

"Two teenage boys in the house and the first one here when there's danger is my nine-year-old daughter. Typical."

He lowered his torch. I lowered my hand.

"As you're here, kindly get your dogs under control. I can't see a damn thing."

I whistled and their ears pricked up. They looked over and I adopted my sternest voice. "Blackie! Vi! Come here."

They stopped splashing and bounded out of the stream. I crouched down to rub their snouts and they shook themselves, spraying cold water from the stream all over me. We walked over to Dad and Argyll.

Dad retrained his torch on the opposite bank of the stream.

"What is it, Dad?"

"That's what I'm trying to see."

I started to scan the bank with my torch too, roving back and forth with the yellow beam.

Back and forth.

Back and forth.

Back and…

Then I saw something.

A reflection?

I went back over the same area.

A reflection. Definitely.

I trained the torch in that one place, peered into its meagre light, stared without blinking until my eyes stung.

I felt the hairs on my arms rise up. My fingers tightened on the torch's rubber casing, vice-like, knuckles white. It shook in my hand involuntarily. Throat and mouth suddenly dry, all I could do was croak, "Dad."

He looked over at me, saw the fear in my face, followed the beam of my torch across the small stretch of water, and brought his own light to bear on the same spot.

In the stronger light of both torches, I could see more clearly.

They looked like skeletons.

Two of them.

Half-buried in reeds at the water's edge.

But while skeletons have no flesh, these two did. Wafer-thin skin stretched so tight it showed every detail of the bones beneath it. Sunken cheeks. Lips like scars. With only the light reflecting from their obscenely bulging eyes to distinguish them from corpses.

Dad set his torch down on the ground and, accompanied by Argyll, plunged into the stream towards them. They took one each, easing them out of the water, cradling them in their arms like bundles of wet rags. As they recrossed the stream, Blackie and Vi leapt up at the pathetic figures, sniffing and pawing at them, but I swiftly brought them to heel. One of the living corpses (male? female? impossible to tell) fixed its eyes on mine as it was carried off. Pity welled up inside me.

Pity. And dread.

Dad and Argyll strode on towards the house without speaking. Then, looking back over his shoulder, Dad said, "Bring my torch."

I picked it up and, Blackie and Vi in tow, fell in behind them.

3

Argyll had been with us for about two years. He was older than my dad, not so tall, but broader across the chest and thicker in the arms. Grey at the temples, he always seemed to have exactly the same amount of stubble on his face. Since we'd moved to the farm, my dad had grown a beard a couple of times, only for it to disappear again shortly afterwards, and it was never quite full. Argyll looked like he grew a full beard every night and had to shave it off again the next morning.

Even with Tom and Rich working alongside him dawn 'til dusk, Dad had been struggling to do all the work needed to keep the farm running. Never mind attempting the repairs to out buildings that had been part of his original plan. Then one day PC Smith, who was a regular visitor by now, strode up the path to the farmhouse with another man. They closeted themselves away in the living room with Dad for the afternoon while us three kids loitered outside (you couldn't really call it 'playing'). Mum wasn't invited to attend so she banged pots and pans about in the kitchen instead (you couldn't really call it 'cooking').

"What do you think that's about?" asked Rich.

"God knows," said Tom. "Perhaps Dad needs someone to help him with the grave digging."

"He looked scary," added Rich.

Eventually, we saw Smith leave by himself and were called back inside. Dad sat us down around the kitchen table and introduced us to the newcomer.

"Everyone, this is Argyll. He's going to be living with us from now on."

Argyll gave a thin-lipped smile and a curt nod.

"He's an old friend of Smithy's, been a farmer most of his life and was a soldier before that. Isn't that right?"

Again, Argyll just nodded.

"He'll be helping out around the place and with the hard work on the farm, which you two should be happy about." Dad looked at Tom and Rich. While Rich made some effort to appear pleased, Tom looked coldly indifferent. "Means you can get back to some studying."

"I think university's out of the question by now, isn't it, Dad?"

Dad gave Tom one of those looks, where his eyes would go glassy and blank, like he wasn't seeing you anymore but looking past you, through you. The switch flicking in his head again.

He composed himself and brought the introductions to a close. "He's also going to help me fix up the barn and is quite happy to sleep in there, so no one has to give up their bedroom." Before adding, pointedly, "Let's all try to make him feel like part of the family."

Argyll looked at each of us in turn as he received a chorus of mumbled 'hellos'. Mum couldn't muster any enthusiasm, real or pretend. But I noticed that, despite the grey hair, the stubble and generally scary exterior, he had kind eyes. The dogs nuzzled up against his legs (which I took as a good sign) and he casually stroked them with his bucket hands. I wondered where his real family was, that he was coming to live with ours. So I hopped down from my chair, walked around the table and formally introduced myself.

"Hello, Argyll, I'm Alice. Welcome to the family."

I put my small hand out to him and he took it in his, engulfing it in a bear-like paw on which the skin was leather-hard. He held my hand like it was a newly laid egg and gently shook it up and down.

He smiled broadly and said, "Why, that's very nice of you indeed, lassie."

Argyll helped Dad rebuild the barn, install the wind turbine and looked after the farm labour when Dad went away with the militia.

Shortly after Argyll joined us, Dad started to leave the farm with Smith, who would arrive in a Police van, pick Dad up and drive him off. Sometimes he'd be away overnight, sometimes even longer. I asked Mum what Dad was doing and she'd only say, "Playing soldier."

Argyll started giving the boys PE classes every morning, which Tom objected to angrily but Rich enjoyed. I'd watch them from my bedroom window, running on the spot, doing push-ups and sit-ups in the front yard, while they gave off great plumes of steamy air on cold mornings and Argyll barked orders at them. I soon got jealous and wanted to join in but Mum was having none of it. She needed my help in the kitchen.

To make up for missing out on PE, Argyll gave me survival lessons. He'd come with me and my brothers for walks in the woods and, while Tom and Rich disappeared up trees or chased one another with sticks, he'd show me how to lay snares, teach me which plants were edible and which weren't, show me how to start a fire without matches.

I loved it all.

Finding a snared rabbit, injured and in pain, was something I never got used to though. "It's the way of the world, lassie," Argyll would say while I held back Blackie and Vi. "All you can do is end the suffering, quick." Then he'd snap the rabbit's neck and tuck it into his satchel.

Watching the dogs leap up at the bag, excited by the scent of blood, I realised how true it was. The small things, the weak and vulnerable things, always seemed to suffer. Even those we love, like I loved my dogs, could be merciless. While to me they were best friends, warm and soft, to a rabbit they were monsters.

And I wished the world was different.

Of course, I had to know more about Argyll so I asked him about his own family, where they were, what had happened to them. He always responded in the fewest words possible.

"Argyll, are you married?"

"I was."

"Where's your wife?"

"She's dead."

A few days later I'd try again.

"Argyll, do you have any children?"

"I did."

"What happened?"

"He died."

A few days after that.

"What was your son's name?"

"Alistair."

"How did he die?"

"Istanbul."

I hadn't heard of that disease before but knew not to push him too far all at once. I was prying in the relentless way children do when they don't realise when it's best to back off and leave well alone.

But one thing I did learn from my pestering of Argyll – grown-ups can be orphans too.

4

Dad and Argyll said nothing as we trudged back up to the farmhouse.

Ahead, I could see Mum silhouetted in the doorway, arms folded across her chest, her winter coat tightly closed over her nightclothes. Arms folded had become her default pose, as if she were saying with her body what she no longer felt at liberty to say out loud. But as we got closer, her pose changed. She dropped her arms, stood suddenly erect and craned her neck. Then she disappeared inside.

A minute later she remerged, arms full of blankets, and hurried towards us. She must have roused the boys too because they appeared in the doorway moments after her and lurked on the threshold, hands stuffed in their coat pockets.

Mum strode towards us, finally breaking into a run when she got close enough to see the piteous state of Dad and Argyll's burden.

"Oh my God, Adam, where did you find them?" she asked, frantically wrapping blankets around the frail bags of bones.

"In the stream."

"Look at you all, you're soaking. And you, Alice?" she only sounded a little bit cross. "Why do you have to go and get involved? It could have been dangerous."

I knew that Mum was worried for me and not really angry. But I didn't need to defend myself as Dad was quick to do it.

"At least one of the children bothers to get involved."

"Where have they come from? Did they say anything?" asked Mum.

Dad shook his head.

We marched single file through the open door, Tom and Rich stepping out of the way to let us pass.

"Not you two," I said to Blackie and Vi as they tried to sneak in after us. "Stay here." They whimpered but did as I told them and stretched out on the ground, covering their noses with their front paws.

"You two idle lumps, make yourselves useful," Dad said irritably. "Rich, you're moving in with Tom, go and get your things. Then the pair of you strip Rich's bed and put clean sheets on it."

"Alice, love," said Mum. "Stay down here with me. We need to boil some water."

Boil some water? I'd helped rescue them! I wanted to go upstairs with the men. Resentfully, I lit the burners on the stove and helped Mum lug pans full of water from the sink over to it. While the water heated, Mum went to the kitchen cupboard where the clean cloths and tea towels were kept. She tucked them under one arm and hefted one of the pans.

"Think you can manage another?" she asked.

I nodded and picked up two smaller pans from the stove.

"Careful now," she added unnecessarily.

I walked behind her up the stairs and followed her along the first-floor landing to the open door of what had been Nuncle and Flick's room, which Rich had eventually inherited a year after Nuncle left. (When Mum finally accepted that he wasn't coming back.) The room was lit by candles. Dad and Argyll had lain the frail figures side by side on top of the bed. The flickering light cast deep shadows, highlighting their sunken cheeks and hollow eyes even more than the torches had.

They looked even more skeletal.

I hated myself for it, but pity had turned to horror.

Horror. And revulsion.

Dad and Argyll stood silently at the foot of the bed, like pall bearers. My father, usually so decisive, so definite, seemed at a loss at what to do next.

Mum carefully placed her pans of hot water on the floor and I did the same. "Okay, you two," she said to Dad and Argyll. "Leave them with me now."

With an air of quiet relief, the two men left the room.

Mum turned to me, "You too, Alice."

I gulped.

"I want to help."

She smiled at me indulgently. "That's very nice of you but, really, there's no need. I can take care of them."

Perhaps I was ashamed of my feelings of horror. Perhaps I was too stubborn to take no for an answer. Perhaps the truth was somewhere in the middle.

"No, I found them. I want to help," I said firmly.

Mum looked dubious. "Okay then, you can stay. But if it gets too much, don't be afraid of telling me so."

I nodded.

"All right then, take this cloth, dip it in the warm water. You can bathe their heads, faces, necks. Gently though. I'll start at their feet. Okay?"

"Okay."

"Let's get going then," said Mum.

The lurching of my stomach told me that perhaps I wasn't okay after all. That perhaps I wasn't as strong as I thought I was.

I dipped the cloth into the water, which was hand-hot but not boiling, wrung it out over the pan to catch the drips, and approached the bed. My hand shook as I raised it to the forehead of the first emaciated figure.

At least this one's eyes were shut.

I gingerly dabbed the cloth along the forehead and the paper-thin skin wrinkled under the pressure of it. I ran the cloth gently down the bridge of the nose and wiped around the nostrils. Beneath the layers of grime, the skin was ashen, grey. I wrung out the cloth in the pan of warm water and returned to the body. I carefully lifted the head, which seemed to weigh almost nothing, and wiped across the crown. Thin wisps of hair came away from the skull and clung to the damp cloth. I barely realised, but I was crying.

Catching myself, I wiped my eyes and nose across the back of my hand, conscious of my tears as a sign of weakness, worried that Mum might see and send me away.

I looked over at her and she was crying too.

And she didn't seem at all ashamed.

I wrung out the cloth to get rid of the hairs then wiped around the mouth, the chin, the neck. On the back of the neck, beneath the layers of filth, I noticed some marks. Lines of different thicknesses and a series of numbers, tattooed at the nape. Like the barcodes on the groceries Mum used to bring home from the supermarket.

I finished wiping the neck, then made my way to the other side of the bed.

"Use a clean cloth, hon," said Mum.

Of course.

I took a clean cloth from the pile and went around the foot of the bed.

This one's eyes were open.

They followed me weakly as I approached the bed, every inch I took towards it like wading through thick mud. I wanted to turn and run from the room but how could I? What would

Mum think of me? So, mouth dry as ashes, I went through the same routine on the second body. All the time, the eyes followed me. And on the nape of the neck, the same marks.

As I wiped around the mouth, I felt it move.

Ever so weakly.

Almost undetectably.

The round, bulging, desperate eyes looked at me even more imploringly. The jaw muscles, so distinct under wafer-thin skin, twitched. I leaned closer, felt a weak exhalation of breath on my cheek.

And in the exhalation, two words.

"Thank you."

I pulled away, tears falling openly now. At the very least I thought they were so weak, so close to death as to be completely unaware of what was going on around them. But knowing that this one knew. Was aware. Could feel. Made it all even more horrible. More than I could bear.

"Mum, I've finished," I said weakly.

She gave me a hug.

"Well done," she said. "You're very brave."

Shoulders shaking as I sobbed, I stumbled from the room, down the corridor, and into the safety of my own bed.

5

I kicked off my boots and let the coat fall from my drooping shoulders onto the bedroom floor. Then I collapsed fully clothed on top of the bed. You think sometimes that what you've seen will stop you from sleeping, but it doesn't. You're too exhausted for the memory of some fresh horror to keep you awake. Instead, it visits you in your dreams.

A sea of scrawny hands and arms is grasping at me, clawing at me, trying to drag me down deeper into them. The arms are just skin stretched tight over bone but their grip is strong. Relentless. Above me there's a bright light and I fight to escape, to pull away from the claw-like hands and get to the light. And then the face of Nuncle. Hollow-cheeked and bulging-eyed, like the faces of the two refugees I'd washed. Nuncle smiles and for a moment he's the old Nuncle, the kind Nuncle, the Nuncle that I know loves me. But then his smile changes, showing row after row of sharp teeth, filed to dagger-like points. My heart thumps like a hammer, so hard I worry it might burst out of my ribcage…

I woke with a jump from the nightmare. I'd worked myself half under the duvet as I slept and had one arm wrapped tightly around the pillow. The thudding in my chest slowly subsided as my mind freed itself of the dream and came back to consciousness. I wondered what had happened to Nuncle, where he was, whether he was safe, whether he missed me like I missed him. I could understand why he'd left us – things had been very, very bad – but part of me resented him for it, felt abandoned.

And all of me missed him.

A lot.

6

Mum didn't wake me to do my chores the next morning. But the kitchen noises disturbed me and I went downstairs anyway.

Everyone else was already there, sitting around the table, finishing off their breakfasts. Mum looked tired and teary; I wondered if she'd left the refugees' bedside at all the previous night. The table was full of breakfast things, and I felt a sudden pang of guilt for the starving people upstairs and who knew how many more out in the world.

"Have they said anything?" I asked. "I could take them some breakfast."

"Just sit down, love, and get your own," said Mum. "We've all had ours."

I began tucking in. The table was sombre and everyone watched me silently as I ate. "What's up?" I asked between mouthfuls of toast. Mum broke the silence.

"The thing is…" Her voice trailed off. She looked over at Dad.

"One of them died, during the night. Mum was worried you'd be upset because you'd helped take care of them."

Of course I was upset. I put the toast down on my plate and started to sniffle.

Mum came and sat next to me, put her arm around my shoulders and rested her cheek on top of my head. "There, there, love."

I caught sight of my brothers as they rolled their eyes at one another and, despite the sadness, felt a rush of anger. I didn't want to give them the satisfaction of seeing me cry so I forced back my tears and said, "Which one?"

"The man. The other one, the woman, the one whose eyes were open, she's still with us, love."

So it was a woman was it? I hadn't been able to tell. Not when they were pulled from the river. Not even while I was washing them.

Dad took over the story in his typically matter-of-fact way. "He was just too weak, been through too much. It's a wonder he wasn't dead when we found them. It's a wonder they both weren't dead."

"Will she be alright?"

"We'll certainly do our best to help her won't we, Adam?" Mum looked over at Dad for confirmation.

Dad looked non-committal. "Well, she can stay here until she's strong enough to be moved," he said. "After that… who knows."

I could feel the tension in Mum's body, a warm wave of anger surging through her and washing over me. Since Nuncle left, she bottled up her feelings most of the time and then, when the pressure got too much, they'd explode from her. I didn't feel tough enough to handle another explosion just now.

"Can I help you with her, Mum?" A small act of consideration, that's all it took to defuse these situations.

"Of course you can, hon." She gave me a kiss on the top of my head. The anger receded, ebbed away, back in its bottle for another day. "But not straight away. There are things I have to do for her first."

I didn't know what kind of things. But knew better than to ask.

After breakfast, Argyll headed into the village and returned with Sergeant (a long overdue promotion, he'd explained) Smith. Inevitably, Tom, Rich and I were ushered outside while the grown-ups held one of their kitchen table conferences. We splashed through the mud in our boots, hands thrust deep in coat pockets, and broke the ice on puddles to occupy ourselves. Blackie and Vi tore around, getting thoroughly muddy in the process.

"What was it like? Touching a dead body, I mean," Rich asked. Why couldn't he ever leave things alone?

"He wasn't dead when I touched him," I answered, defiantly.

"Do you think she'll die too? The starving woman?"

"Careful, Rich," said Tom, "or you might get another of Alice's kicks in the bollocks."

The memory wasn't exactly fresh but, even so, the incident had never been forgotten. Boys can be quite sensitive about these things, apparently. I stood a little taller and eyed Rich as threateningly as I could. He backed off and started whacking at a particularly thick bit of puddle ice with a stick.

"What do you think it means, Tom? Her coming here?" Tom was the person I trusted the most to know things.

"It means that Dad was right."

Rich stopped his war with the ice and looked over at Tom. I was too surprised to say anything. Tom was the focus of our discontent. If there was something we didn't like about the farm and the new life we'd been thrust into, it was Tom who voiced it. He'd stood up to Dad so many times it had almost become a joke. He was the family rebel, the firstborn son defying the father.

Rich and me just stared and waited for him to explain this sudden conversion.

"Don't you get it? Britain doesn't have starving people. It certainly didn't used to. There was poverty, of course there was, and people begged for food, but even they weren't starving. Not like this. And if two of them can get here, to the middle of nowhere, imagine what it must be like out there," he gestured with his head beyond the earthworks, beyond the stream, out into the big wide world we'd left behind. "In the cities and the towns. There could be thousands, hundreds of thousands, of people roaming the countryside, desperate and hungry. Dying on their feet. Dad brought us here cos he saw it coming."

We both continued to stare at him.

"Dad was right."

I felt realisation dawn on me. I'd been too young to question my parents' decision to uproot the family. Sure, there were things I missed about my old life, but I hadn't been old enough to understand what I was leaving behind. For my brothers, it was different. They were about to go to big school. Tom in particular already had a clear idea of what he wanted to do with his life. All that had been taken away from them, the possibility of what life would offer reduced to a freezing cold farmhouse with crumbling out buildings and a few muddy acres, hundreds of miles from home. Is it any wonder Tom was bitter? So to hear this from him, of all people, made it that much more significant.

Dad was right.

If we hadn't got out when we did it could have been our half-starved, half-naked bodies in a ditch somewhere.

Dad was right.

I don't know how long we would have stood pondering this but Mum appeared in the farmhouse doorway and called us in for lunch. We trudged back up to the farmhouse in silence, each of us deep in thought. (Well, I was, and Tom always was. I can't be sure about Rich.) Ahead of us, Argyll emerged from the farmhouse carrying a shovel and casually walked towards the orchard.

"It looks like you were right, too," said Rich.

Tom glanced at Rich, puzzled.

"About Dad needing help to dig the graves."

7

When we entered the kitchen, Sergeant Smith, Mum and Dad were sitting at the table.

"Sit down, kids," said Dad. We dutifully took our places.

"Who is she?" asked Tom.

"We don't know," said Dad.

"We'll find out, soon enough," Smith added pointedly.

"The most important question isn't who she is, but how did she get here? And how many more of them might be coming. You know I'm part of the local militia?"

Dad in the militia? The boys nodded. Hold on a minute, I didn't know anything about this. Did everyone know except me?

"And that I go out on patrol with them from time to time?"

Again, nods from the boys. Playing soldier. So that was what Mum had meant. What, was I too young to be told? I wasn't a little girl anymore, I was ten. I decided to have a good sulk about being kept in the dark and folded my arms across my chest.

"Well, after this, we need to increase the number of patrols. Winter's on us, which will make people more desperate."

"Aye, it will also kill off a lot of them," said Smith with a brutal bluntness that nobody, not even Mum, objected to.

"They won't all be weak and helpless and like the two upstairs. Some will be armed and dangerous. I don't want to be away from the farm more than I have to. Especially now. Argyll can't do everything and I'm needed here to keep our home secure. So... Tom, Rich. You're old enough now. I want you to join the patrols. A lot of young men from the villages are joining up too. Argyll's made sure you're fit enough and you know the area like the back of your hand. What do you say?"

Tom looked at Rich, Rich beamed back at Tom.

Rich was overjoyed. "Really, Dad? Can we? That's awesome."

Dad smiled at his youngest son. Then turned his attention to his oldest. "What about you, Tom?"

Tom's response was, typically, more measured but took both my parents by surprise. "Of course, Dad. If I can help defend our home, I will."

Where was the argument? The resistance? The questioning of Dad's decisions?

Dad looked genuinely pleased. Mum looked anxious.

"You know, Tom, no one's forcing you," she said.

"I know, Mum. But Dad can't be everywhere. I'm old enough. I want to help."

"Well, that was easy," said Smith, standing. "Great news. I'll head back and add their names to the roster. I'll issue an updated patrol schedule tomorrow and we'll take it from there."

Smith put on his coat, picked up his shotgun, made ready to leave. He shook Dad's hand and then the hands of the boys. He'd not done that before.

"What about me?" I asked.

"You want a handshake too, lassie?" asked Smith.

"No. What about me going on patrol?"

Smith smiled and ruffled my hair. I pulled my head back crossly. Mum and Dad smiled, my brothers scoffed.

"Now don't be silly, dear. You're far too young," said Mum.

"And far too girl," said Rich.

"Who was first out of bed last night? You two were fast asleep while I was protecting the farm."

"That was different, Alice," said Mum. "The patrols are dangerous. They go looking for trouble. Not waiting for it to come to us."

I calmed down and quietly seethed. As Smith left, Argyll came back in from the orchard. They exchanged a terse greeting.

"Argyll."

"Stuart."

Argyll's hands were covered in soil. He went to the sink and washed them clean.

8

Mum wouldn't let me go up and see her that first day. She'd said there were things she wanted to do for her first and I hadn't understood. But on the second day she let me join her after breakfast. I was nervous about seeing the woman again, but I needn't have been.

Mum had been busy.

She'd washed her lank hair, dressed her in an old, heavily patched dress, put lipstick on her, and blusher, and eye shadow. At first I thought this was for my benefit, to make her less scary. (Not that it worked as the make-up on her hollowed-out face made her look bizarre, almost like a clown.) But I was wrong anyway.

Mum hadn't done it for me. She'd done it for the woman.

To make her feel human again.

I could see it had worked, at least a little. Because there seemed to be an inner light shining out from her bulging eyes as they followed me around the room.

Mum had me sit on the edge of the bed and spoon feed warm water into the woman's mouth. I coaxed water in while those big, bulging eyes stared back at me, as if she were permanently surprised. Meanwhile, Mum gave the woman a bed bath, chatting to her gently all the time, describing what she was doing so as not to alarm her.

Now if you should ever, and I hope against hope that you don't, but if you should ever have to nurse someone back from the edge of starvation, from the edge of death, there's one very important thing you need to know.

Don't feed them.

It sounds crazy, I know.

Surely the thing they need most urgently is food.

But if I had gone upstairs and given breakfast to the woman that first morning, I would have killed her.

Because at the furthest reaches of starvation, you're too weak to chew. You're too weak to digest. Your stomach shrinks and your muscles are eaten up by your body, cannibalising itself in a desperate search for energy. The heart is just another muscle so it gets weak as well and suddenly reintroducing food can actually cause the poor, starving person you're trying to save to die from a heart attack.

I don't know how Mum knew this but she did. Where I would have blundered in, spooning porridge and cereal into the woman's mouth, Mum made certain that we took it slowly.

Infinite care.

Infinite patience.

Day after day, little by little.

At first, only water, boiled and left to cool to reduce the risk of bacteria finishing the job that famine had started. Water with a little bit of sugar dissolved into it to give her just enough energy to start the long process of the body healing itself.

Then, once she'd rehydrated, a few porridge oats were stirred in with the sugar. "Gruel," my mum called it. "It's what they used to give to children for supper if they'd been naughty."

I decided never to be naughty enough to earn a diet of gruel.

Slowly, the gruel was thickened into something closer to porridge.

Slowly, the woman's stomach got used to larger amounts of food.

Slowly, her hollow cheeks filled out. Her bulging eyes settled back into their sockets.

By the third week, Mum was happy to let me feed breakfast to the woman alone. I perched on the side of the bed as I'd done before and, trying to be as chirpy as I could, began to slowly spoon the porridge into her mouth.

"Here we go, open wide."

Her mouth worked laboriously around each mouthful. I sat patiently and waited for her to swallow. As I offered her the next mouthful, she started to work her lips, as if trying to form words. Her eyes pleaded with me to move closer and I leaned in, turning my head towards the faint sounds coming from her open mouth. But they were too faint and I couldn't make out what she was trying to say.

"Sorry, what did you say?"

With a huge effort of will, she tried again, her voice barely above a whisper.

"Claire."

"Claire? Is that what you said?"

She closed her eyes by way of confirmation, gave the faintest of nods.

"Your name's Claire?"

Another faint nod.

"I'm Alice. Alice Fox. You're safe now, with us."

Her chest heaved up and down as she readied herself for the effort of speaking again. I leaned even closer.

"John," she whispered.

This meant nothing to me.

"Sorry, who's John?"

She rolled her eyes to her left, to the other side of the bed, the side where the man had lain on the night we found them.

The side where the man had died later that night.

I felt my mouth go dry.

"Was John your friend?"

Again, the faintest of nods from her.

"I'm sorry, Claire but… but John died."

She closed her eyes. A sigh escaped her. Then, with her eyes still closed, she whispered, "Lucky."

"Yes, you are lucky. We're looking after you now."

Her eyes flickered open. One final effort from her, the faintest of whispers.

"Not me. Him."

She fell silent. The blinds of her eyelids drew down. Exhausted from the effort of speaking, she fell asleep, her thin chest rising and falling rhythmically. For a while, I remained still, not wanting to disturb her. Then I quietly left the room.

Mum heard me entering the kitchen. "Everything alright?" she asked without looking up from the sink.

"Here name's Claire." She looked up now. "The lady upstairs, here name's Claire," I repeated.

"She spoke to you?" I nodded. "What else did she say?"

"That the man's name was John. That was all, before she went back to sleep." I decided not to mention that she'd thought John lucky to be dead.

Mum looked concerned. Then her expression softened as if she'd decided this was good news. She went back to the washing up. "It's good that she's getting stronger," she said. "Maybe you should give her breakfast by yourself every day from now on? As she's getting used to you, she might open up a bit more."

I was happy to do it. It was me who first spotted her in the river that night and I felt, not so much a sense of duty, more a sense of ownership. If she was going to speak to anyone, it was going to be me.

"But let's keep this between ourselves for now, eh, love," Mum said. "Don't mention it to your brothers. Or your Dad. They'll only pester her and she's not strong enough for that yet."

"Of course, Mum." I took this at face value. I liked the idea of Mum and me sharing a secret, of knowing something that the boys didn't.

They'd not told me about Dad being in the militia. Now it was my turn.

9

At first she could barely sit up in bed but, with Mum and me taking care of her and keeping the menfolk away as best we could, she was soon able to hobble from the room.

Make it downstairs.

Make it outside (when it wasn't too cold).

By late spring she was taking a morning walk with me and the dogs. Just to the bottom of the field and back. Wrapped up warm, of course, and only when there wasn't frost in the air or damp underfoot.

By early summer she was helping Mum with the chores. I know Dad wanted her out because Mum had told me. "He says she's a 'security risk'. Ridiculous!" she'd complained. "'Another bloody mouth to feed' he said. I had to tell him that if she was kicked out, I was going too."

"And me, Mum."

It earned me a hug.

"I've been cooking and cleaning and looking after this dirty old house by myself since, well, since Flick. I know you're getting bigger, hon, and you do what you can but, even so, Claire will be very helpful."

Her name was Claire White and she was twenty-seven years old. To my eyes, she looked ancient but being close to death had added another twenty years to her face. The man we found her with, John, was her husband and they came from a large town in the middle of England called Derby. (I vaguely remembered hearing of it when I was little but couldn't picture the map of England in my head anymore.)

Claire had a job as something called a 'receptionist' and her husband was a mechanic. They had one child together.

A daughter.

Claire never could bring herself to tell me her name.

Things in Derby had become very dangerous. There were riots for food, no electricity and no heating in their flat. So, one day, Claire and John put their daughter and as many of their things as they could into their car and left. They couldn't go South, East or West, because there were big cities in all of those directions where life was even worse. They went North instead (much like we had), along the smaller roads, winding their way through an area called the Peak District. John's family were from a smaller town, Buxton, and even though he'd not heard from them in a while he hoped that things wouldn't be as bad as in the big towns and cities.

John had been saving their petrol ration and had enough to get them to Buxton but no further. It was only about twenty miles. But they hadn't got that far when they came to a roadblock where armed men turned them out of their vehicle. They weren't soldiers or police but they said they were in charge now. They took the car for the petrol and all their possessions. Claire and John were left with enough food for a couple of days, and the men only left them that because they had the baby. Even so, Claire told me, they had been lucky. Armed men were doing much worse things to people.

They carried on toward Buxton, now on foot. When they reached the edge of the town they realised it was hopeless to enter. Buildings were on fire and they could hear gunshots, people screaming. The small towns had been overrun.

They kept going across country, kept heading North, away from the big cities. They slept on the ground in woods and copses, under hedges, by stone walls, in abandoned farmhouses and barns. They tried to stay out of sight and hid when other people came close.

The baby was very small and Claire could feed her but sometimes, especially at night, she would cry and this made John frightened. People might hear her and find their hiding place.

"Wouldn't they have helped you? Because of the baby, I mean?" I asked.

"The opposite," said Claire.

The food they'd been left with soon ran out so they scavenged from hedgerows, in abandoned buildings, burned-out shops. They clawed at the ground in fields and dug up whatever they could find. John climbed trees for eggs from birds' nests. "We were lucky it was summer or we wouldn't have lasted a week," said Claire.

One day they came across a potato field and John filled their bags with as many as they could carry. ("We eat a lot of potatoes here," I confided, worried she might be sick of them now.) But when they ran out, for days, there was nothing. Claire's milk dried up and the baby went hungry. She cried and cried, but there was nothing Claire could do.

They'd been on the road for weeks now. Hope seemed lost and they might just as well lie down and die. Which is what they were doing, in a ditch by a dry stone wall. Morning had come and they were shivering in the first light when they heard the sound of an engine turning over nearby. And again. And again. Men's voices were raised and there was a lot of shouting.

With his last strength, John crawled from the ditch, over the wall and onto the road. There was an army truck carrying refugees. It was falling behind the rest of the column because the engine wouldn't start but, as he was a mechanic, he promised to fix it if they'd take his family with them. Weak as he was, John got the truck started and the soldiers in charge kept their promise.

Claire lay where she was with the baby, waiting for them both to die. She stared hard at her daughter, trying to fix her image in her mind, the piercing blue eyes of an infant, the thin wisps of hair waiting to thicken into a moppet's blonde locks. Her daughter's eyes flickered and closed, "Just sleeping, I hoped." Then booted feet appeared either side of Claire's head and she was hoisted into the air.

She was put in the back of a covered truck crowded with people. An old woman gave her water and a piece of dry bread and she fell asleep. "Another hour in that ditch and I'd have been dead, I'm sure of it," Claire told me.

"And what about your baby?"

It took the longest time for Claire to give up this detail. Eventually she told me that the soldiers who carried her onto the truck had left her baby daughter's body in the ditch where she'd been found.

Her tiny, shrivelled body left for the rats and foxes.

A tiny spark of hope.

Extinguished.

The truck trundled on all that day and into the night. The other refugees shared what scraps of food they had with them, and John and Claire began to feel stronger. Each refugee had their own story of horror or heartbreak. Of dead families, dead children, bloodshed and desperation. They were taken to a refugee camp at an old army base in Yorkshire. 'Cat-Trick' Claire called it but I knew that couldn't be right. For refugees like John and Claire there was the chance of shelter and food but the others told them that there were different kinds of camps, too.

"Internment camps," Claire said.

"What are those?"

"That's where they put undesirables."

"What's an undesirable?"

"Criminals. Terrorists. Anyone who doesn't agree with the government."

The undesirables in the internment camps didn't agree with one another either so they fought among themselves. Or were beaten, tortured or starved to death by the guards.

The Cat-Trick refugee camp was their last hope. They arrived late at night and were 'processed'. They had to prove their own identity and their personal details were logged on a computer. Each new arrival was then given a barcode, tattooed on the back of the neck, that could be scanned to quickly identify who they were.

Far from salvation, the refugee camp was a hellish place. Tens of thousands of people were herded into it, guarded by watchtowers, barbed wire and armed soldiers, but otherwise left to fend for themselves inside. Between the walls of canvas and plastic sheeting, sewage flowed in the streets. Disease was everywhere. There was a curfew and anyone caught outside their tent after dark was labelled an 'undesirable' and shot on sight. Yes, there was food, but not enough to go around so people fought as they had on the streets of Derby for a stale crust or tin can. "You have no idea what people are prepared to do to stay alive for one more day," she told me.

They couldn't stay in the refugee camp. They couldn't endure it.

Claire begged John and, pockets stuffed with a few bits of food they'd manage to save, they waited for night and, with a group of about twenty others, went through the wire.

Machine gunshots rang out from the watchtowers as they sprinted across the no man's land outside the camp. But, while the other refugees fell, they ran on. Stumbling on together in the pitch dark.

Still heading North, they kept moving. Dodging army patrols, armed militias and any other refugees they came across.

Their food ran out so they scavenged what they could, ate dead things they found in ditches. But winter was drawing on and, as the ground became hard from the frost, they couldn't dig into farmers' fields or even unearth worms to eat.

Hunger ate at them from the inside.

But they crawled on.

On the very brink of death, they found a stream.

And that's when I found them.

That was Claire's story, put back together from the fragments she gave me. The final piece fell into place one morning beside the grave in the orchard where Argyll had buried John. It was marked by a flat stone and a rough wooden cross. We stood by it, holding hands, for the longest time.

After an age she broke the silence. "The worst thing in the world is watching the ones you love shrivel up in front of your eyes and not being able to do anything about it."

"You're safe now," I said.

She hugged me tight then. I must have sounded ridiculous.

Because, by then, even my young mind had worked it out.

The farm, this place, was an island.

A tiny speck of land in a sea of horror.

A piece of driftwood from a shipwreck.

How long could we continue to cling onto it? God alone knew.

10

I came downstairs dressed for outdoors and dashed through the kitchen.

"Mum, I'm going to check the snares."

"Okay, hon, don't go too far. Take the dogs."

"Don't I always? Claire, are you coming?"

It was spring now and Claire was strong enough to help Mum with kitchen chores. I made it my mission to encourage her out of the farmhouse into the fresh air as often as I could. She looked at Mum for confirmation.

"Of course it's okay. Off you go."

"Thanks, ma'am," she mumbled.

"Claire, please stop calling me 'ma'am'. I'm not royalty. I'm Julia."

"Sorry... Julia."

I clambered into my coat, took down the polka-dot rucksack that had come with me from St Albans, and threw it on my back. I used to cart my toys around in it but they had all been lost, broken or abandoned long since. The bag, though, was waterproof inside and out, a bit worn at the edges but perfect for carrying the animals caught in my snares. Claire pulled on Flick's old overcoat, which swamped her tiny frame, turned up the cuffs and we were ready to go.

Once outside, I untied the dogs and petted them furiously. God, they were gorgeous. Always excited to see me, excited to be free of their tethers, immediately alert, coats glistening, tails wagging, eyes shining. Their warm breath mingled with mine as I knelt down and nuzzled them.

Claire stood off at a distance.

"Come on, Claire, they won't hurt you."

There had been guard dogs at the internment camp. Mean dogs. She'd seen them do things she wouldn't tell me about.

"Blackie and Vi aren't like the camp dogs. They wouldn't hurt a fly. Would you?"

I rubbed my face against theirs, warm and wet.

Claire made no move towards them.

Eventually, I thought. *She'll learn to trust them eventually.*

We splashed through mud and puddles down to the edge of the field. I chatted all the way. Claire, as always, said little. She walked with me as far as the bottom of the field. The perimeter of the property was as far as she would go, not confident enough yet to step beyond it. She'd developed the habit of seeing me off and waiting for me to return with my catch.

"Bye, Claire. Come on, you two." The dogs scrambled over the wall with me.

"Bye, Alice. Be careful."

"Why does everyone keep saying that?" I said crossly without feeling cross at all. It was nice to have people who cared.

I quickly disappeared into the tangle of trees that surrounded the farm. The small wood had been a playground for me and my brothers when we were younger and now it was a very useful larder. We'd done well for food so far; pork, eggs, chicken, potatoes, vegetables from Mum's garden and fruit from the orchard met our day-to-day needs. Dad traded pigs and sacks of potatoes for essentials like flour and we got our butchering done in return for a cut of the meat. In the autumn, a hedgerow harvest yielded blackberries for fruit pies and jams. And Argyll had shown us which mushrooms were safe to eat and which weren't. Even so, my snares were a good source of extra meat. A bit of rabbit or squirrel made a welcome change from pig, pig, pig.

It was cool under the canopy, dark despite the bright spring morning and damp with dew underfoot. Small animal tracks were dotted around here and there. Despite the birdsong, most of the noise came from my welly-booted feet and the dogs, who panted heavily and tore off ahead of me through underbrush and bracken before circling round and coming back to heel.

My snares were expertly placed, well hidden from their prey but positioned on the runs that the animals used most frequently. Argyll had shown me how to find a good spot. Trampled undergrowth, droppings and tufts of fur were clear signs that wildlife regularly went that way. But the animals were smart, too, and would become wary of a route too heavily scented by people and dogs, so you had to move your snares around to stay one step ahead of them. Doing that meant poachers would struggle to find the snares too, which could only be a good thing.

I moved steadily from snare to snare, deeper and deeper into the woods. The rucksack was filling up nicely. Two rabbits and two squirrels was already a good morning's work. I squatted down on my haunches and felt through the undergrowth for the next snare, parting the wet grass with my hands.

There was a sudden flurry of movement, inches away from my nose. Surprised, I fell backwards onto the earth.

The dogs leapt forward, inquisitively sniffing and snarling. I sat up and pulled them back.

"Blackie! Vi! Come away now."

The dogs did as they were told and I leant forward, peering into the undergrowth. There was another explosive flurry of movement but, this time, I was ready for it. I pushed apart the foliage and found the snare. Caught in it was a rabbit, not yet full grown. Its hind leg had been snared and it twitched and lunged desperately.

Usually, an animal goes through a snare headfirst and it closes around their neck, choking and killing them quickly. Their instinct is to struggle to free themselves and this just makes the end come even quicker.

This rabbit, though, had managed to get its leg trapped. The snare's lethally thin wire had cut into it but not too deeply. There was enough blood to get the dogs excited but, looking at it, I knew the rabbit would be okay if I released it.

Of course, I could have just broken its neck; I'd done that dozens of times. But something in the rabbit's desperate struggle for freedom stopped me. I positioned my legs either side of its body, pinioning it with my thighs.

"Calm down, poor thing."

It thrashed around even more violently so I closed my legs tighter while I carefully worked the snare's wire loose. Careful in case it cut into the rabbit's leg deeper. And careful so as not to cut my own fingers to ribbons.

"Hold still now," I said pointlessly, "you're not helping." The stench of human and dog must have been terrifying for the tiny, twitching bundle.

Within a few moments, the wire was loose enough for the thrashing hind leg to come free. "There you go," I said, standing and releasing the rabbit. Its injury really wasn't bad because, instantly, it sprang away.

The dogs sprang after it.

"Blackie! Vi!" I shouted at their tails as they disappeared from sight, deep into the undergrowth. They'd got a scent of blood and would chase the rabbit until the scent was lost or they got bored. I hoped they wouldn't catch the poor thing and make freeing it a waste of time.

It took me a moment to realise, but I was utterly alone.

Normally this wouldn't have bothered me in the slightest but, for some strange reason, I felt threatened.

Like I was being watched.

The woods were dark and humid and strangely silent. And why weren't the birds singing?

Then a dry branch cracked sharply behind me and I spun around, heart pounding like the poor, snared rabbit's. Out of the corner of my eye I glimpsed a shadowy figure disappearing behind a tree.

I'm sure I did.

Or was it my imagination?

"Who's there?"

The surrounding forest was as still as a churchyard.

"Come out. I saw you."

There was movement up ahead of me. Then, from behind a tree, a large figure emerged. It was dark in this part of the woods, the man's face was in shadow.

And I was afraid.

I made ready to run.

The man moved closer and I made out his features in the dappled light.

"Oh, it's you, Argyll." My thumping heart subsided. "What are you doing here?"

He didn't answer straight away but continued slowly walking towards me. I noticed he was carrying a thick length of tree branch.

"I wanted to see how you were getting on with those snares," he said. Funny, I'd been checking snares by myself for ages. What was so special about today?

He walked slowly towards me, brandishing the branch like a club.

Then the bushes either side of me exploded in a mass of panting fur as Blackie and Vi bounded back from their chase. They whimpered, circled me, licked my fingers. I was pleased to see them, strangely relieved, even though it was only Argyll. Pleased, too, that their snouts were unbloodied.

"Hello, you two," I said as casually as I could.

The dogs started barking at Argyll. I knelt down beside them, stroked them, tried to calm them down. "Hey, what's with this noise? It's Argyll. We know him, don't we?"

Did we?

The dogs' barks turned into snarls. They bared their teeth, eyes fixed on Argyll. I didn't know why but my heart started to pound again.

The tension was broken by raised voices.

"Hey, you two!"

"Woo hoo!"

Tom and Rich. Back from night patrol. Their camouflage gear specked with mud and each with a shotgun slung across their back.

They jogged down a tree-covered rise, snapping twigs and branches as they came. It certainly wasn't a stealth patrol they'd been on. But the dogs stopped snarling and greeted the boys with typical enthusiasm.

"What are you doing, checking snares?" asked Rich.

"Your powers of observation have become razor-sharp since you joined the militia," I replied.

"We were taking a shortcut back to the farm when we heard Blackie and Vi," said Tom. "Thought we'd come find you." Picking up on the odd atmosphere he added, "Everything okay?"

"Fine. Just fine," I said. "I was going home too, when Argyll appeared."

"Well then, we can all go home together," said Rich.

I was relieved. I couldn't say why. But I decided it might be best not to spend time alone with Argyll from now on.

We headed off through the woods, back to the farm, the boys chatting excitedly. Argyll followed on behind us in silence.

11

"We went over the ridge of hills towards Ecclefechan, as far as Loch Earn. There was smoke coming from that direction, so we went to investigate." Rich was babbling with excitement around a mouthful of toast.

He'd been on night patrol with Tom but had come back in time for breakfast.

The world may have been falling apart but trust my brothers not to miss their breakfast.

By now the boys were experienced hands when it came to patrols. At first they'd only been allowed out in daylight and for a few hours at a time. However, as they'd come to no harm and got more familiar with the terrain around the farm, they'd been allowed to go out longer and later. Night patrols were now an accepted part of the routine.

As was 'reporting back' to Dad. As far as I was concerned, it should have been called 'showing off'. Dad would sit at the breakfast table with a look of intense concentration on his face. Occasionally he'd make notes or get them to go back over something but, listening in as I did, there didn't seem much to tell. The biggest threat to Tom and Rich in their first few months seemed to have come from the weather.

But, even by Rich's excitable standards, this report back had more to it than the usual ones.

"We approached from the South and kept ourselves out of sight. Ain't that right, Tom?"

Tom nodded. He was already a patrol leader and, in contrast to Rich, tended to be quiet and thoughtful afterwards, only contributing to the report with key details that Rich, in his excitement, was liable to forget.

"We crept up behind some boulders and Tom peeked out over them. Then he ordered the advance…"

"All I said was, 'come on'," Tom corrected.

"Whatever. So we went down and found, well, it looked like there'd been a big battle." Rich was almost breathless.

"Is that right, Tom?" asked Dad.

"I wouldn't say a big battle. More like a skirmish. There were half a dozen burned out vehicles, some military, some not. They had bullet holes in them."

"There were bodies too, Dad," Rich continued.

"How many?" Dad was taking notes now.

"I counted six," said Tom. "And three wounded survivors."

Dad looked up. Mum stopped what she was doing, came over and sat down at the table with us. Claire paused at the sink where she was washing up the breakfast things.

"What did you do about the survivors?" asked Mum.

The boys exchanged a serious look. Rich was good at the exciting stuff but not so good when difficult questions needed to be answered.

After a moment, Tom stepped in. "What could we do? There were too many of them and too few of us. We went back to the command post…"

"As quickly as we could…" cut in Rich.

"As quickly as we could," continued Tom, "and informed Captain Smith."

Command post?

Captain Smith?

When I'd first met Smith he'd been a plain old police constable and it wasn't five minutes since he'd been promoted (or had promoted himself) to sergeant.

But rank in the militia had nothing to do with what you did in real life.

The village butcher called himself Lieutenant Cross. He'd even changed the sign outside his shop. Dad would say, "Thanks, Lieutenant," when we went to collect the pig meat. For the last four years it had been a simple, "Thanks, Brian."

At least Dad wasn't going around calling himself 'Colonel This' or 'Major That'.

Not yet, anyway.

"What did Smith do?" Mum asked. She couldn't bring herself to call him Captain.

"*Captain* Smith thanked us for our report and said he'd send out a patrol right away," said Tom.

"And did he?"

"I don't know, Mum. We came home."

"Why wouldn't he? The survivors would have valuable intelligence," said Rich.

"And they'd need help," Tom added.

Mum looked at Dad. "I just want to make sure that my sons, *my* sons..." her voice was rising, "didn't leave wounded people to die."

"Of course he would have sent a patrol out, Julia," said Dad. "He'd be a lousy captain if he didn't."

Mum couldn't let it go. "To help them though, the survivors. Not to gather intelligence." She said 'gather intelligence' like it was dirt in her mouth.

"It is possible, you know, to do both," said Dad. There was a moment of heavy silence. "Anyway, what could they do?" He gestured at my brothers. "There's only four to a patrol. Three survivors. They couldn't have carried them. And if they had moved them, they might have made their injuries worse."

Dad's words had a firm logic that seemed to calm Mum down. She rose from her seat at the table and returned to her post next to Claire at the kitchen sink. Claire, head down, resumed washing up.

"Okay, boys, well done, off to bed now." Dad dismissed them. They stood, ran out of the room and clattered upstairs.

Dad stood and grabbed his coat from the hook on the back of the kitchen door. "I'm going into the village to catch up with Smithy." The outside door creaked as he exited, letting in a cold draught of early morning April air. The latch clicked back into place and I heard him yell for Argyll.

"Do you think it's silly, Mum?" I asked. "All this playing at war?"

"Enough boys play at war, they'll start one."

Mum hadn't said this.

Claire had.

Surprised, Mum and I looked over at her.

Getting her to talk about everything she'd lived through had, understandably, been a slow process. Even since she'd got stronger (she would never fully recover) and started helping Mum, she never spoke above a whisper. Rarely said more than two or three words at a time.

She pulled the plug from the kitchen sink and the water gurgled as it drained away. She turned to us, drying her hands on her apron.

"It's inevitable," she said.

12

It was Easter Sunday on the fourth anniversary of our arrival, just a few weeks after my tenth birthday, and we made the pilgrimage into the village to go to church. Even Claire joined us, coaxed beyond the walls of the farm by my urging. "You've done so well," I said, "come so far. There's really nothing to be frightened of. It's only a trip to church. Everyone's really friendly. Otherwise, won't you get lonely by yourself in the farmhouse?"

I think it was the last argument that convinced her. The fear of the outside world. Or the fear of being left behind in an old, isolated farmhouse. So, gingerly, squeezing my hand tightly, Claire stepped beyond the stone wall that marked the perimeter of the farm and onto the path leading to the village.

"Well done, Claire, you're doing great." I encouraged her every few minutes. But not once did she relax. Not once did she let go of my hand.

It was a dreary day and Dad lead the way in silence. He would normally be irritable on the walk into the village, annoyed if the rest of us were too slow, urging any stragglers to keep up, or ticking off Tom and Rich if they were messing around too much.

But not this time. Tom and Rich weren't with us. They were part of a patrol that was keeping an eye on the house while we were absent.

At one point I increased the pace and dragged Claire up alongside Dad. "Claire's being very brave isn't she?" I said. But he didn't respond. Not out of rudeness, he simply didn't hear me. He was lost in his own thoughts, his eyes fixed on the path ahead.

The cloud seemed even lower, the day even greyer during the walk and a little drizzle started to fall. Our little column filed through the churchyard. The gravestones stood out at various heights and angles like broken teeth, all of them grey as the sky. Not a single daffodil dared poke its yellow head out of the saturated earth. I hoped that spring, real spring, would come soon.

When we entered, the church was packed, with more people than I'd ever seen before, even at Christmas. We had to share a pew by the door near the back of the church. I ended up separated from Mum and Dad, wedged between Claire and Argyll, who I'd been wary of ever since the incident in the woods. But if he'd noticed I'd been keeping my distance from him, he didn't let on.

Maggie and her grandma were sitting in the row in front of me. Her blonde hair was neatly combed and pulled into a ponytail and she wore a crisp, cotton dress with large red flowers on it. I felt self-conscious in my heavily patched jeans (pulled in at the waist with one of Rich's old belts) and home-knit jumper. But we were a farming family now, not townies, and I would have bet she couldn't set a snare to save her life. She was, though, the only girl of my own age that I knew so I went out of my way to say 'Hi' whenever I saw her.

I leaned across Claire and tapped Maggie on the shoulder. "Hello, Maggie, you look pretty. How are you?"

She looked over and smiled, genuinely pleased to see me. "Hi, Alice. I've not seen you in ages."

"We've been busy on the farm."

"Well, now it's spring, you should come into town more. Nan will be happy to make us both tea. Won't you, Nan?"

Her grandma looked around. "Oh, hello, Alice. Of course you can come for tea. Any time you like."

"Thanks, I'll have to ask my mum, but I'm sure it will be fine." I gave Maggie my best smile. It would be nice to have a proper girl friend. I mean, I liked the woods and the stream and the fields. And I adored my dogs. But an actual girl friend might make up for all the talk of soldiers, militias and insurgents that Dad and my brothers made me listen to.

A chord on the organ announced the appearance of the vicar. He took his place in the pulpit, said a few things about Jesus, then introduced Smith.

(PC? Sergeant? Captain? I couldn't keep track anymore.)

Smith strode up the aisle in his policeman's uniform, buttons gleaming, cap tucked under one arm. He looked very official. He climbed to the pulpit, cleared his throat, and addressed the congregation.

"Good day, everyone. Happy Easter."

"Happy Easter, Smithy," a few people replied, good-naturedly. On the other side of Argyll, my dad watched him intently.

"As you know, I'm head of the militia hereabouts. And I work with other militias in the district, sharing intelligence and coordinating our response to potential threats to our lives and homes."

Murmurs of acknowledgement and approval.

"Last week, a patrol lead by young Tom Rogers…" Heads turned towards where we were sitting."…discovered the site of a recent fire fight between Scottish army regulars and rebel insurgents. Under interrogation, the surviving rebels revealed their numbers and their positions. Then they were tried and executed."

Cries of 'here, here' and 'well done, Smithy' rang around the church. Smithy raised his hands to quiet everyone down again.

"Rest assured, ladies and gentlemen, that coordinated action to smoke out these rebels and remove the threat they pose will take place in the very near future."

The cheers grew in volume. As they died away, Smith wound up his contribution.

"Anyway, that's all the local news from me. Now we have a guest speaker. Someone who came to live among us only a few short years ago but who, along with his family, has already made a huge contribution to the community. Alan Rogers."

Surprised, I looked along the pew to Dad, who stepped out into the aisle and walked to the front of the church. He'd not said anything about this, at least not to me. But, as I was learning, I was always the last to know.

Dad shook hands with Smith and climbed up into the pulpit. He fumbled inside his jacket pocket for a sheaf of papers, unfolded them, smoothed them out. Then he coughed into his hand once... twice... and began to speak. Uncertainly at first but with growing confidence the longer he went on.

"Good morning, everyone, happy Easter. I was asked by Reverend Haigh and Sergeant... sorry, Captain Smith to say a few words today, about my family and our experiences, and what brought us... you might say drove us... to come and live among you.

"In case you weren't aware, Britain is on its knees. These islands, that once ran the world, are financially and morally bankrupt. Our last strength has been spent fighting other people's wars while the real war, all along, was here at home.

First the cities tore themselves apart. Nottingham. Liverpool. Leeds. As you know, London is burning. The towns soon followed. Their streets, rivers of blood. Oldham. Walsall. Slough. Names that have become a byword for the worst depravity people can do to each another. The villages, villages like ours, will inevitably be next."

Dad's speech was interrupted with outbursts of support from the congregation. Cries of 'here, here' and 'that's right' and 'Amen' resounded around the church. I'd never seen, or heard, anything like it. When the vicar gave a sermon, apart from the occasional snore, you could hear a pin drop.

Inspired by the encouragement, Dad was getting into his stride.

"Foreign elements who hate our way of life and everything that we love were given shelter, housed and schooled at the expense of decent people. Degenerates were given free rein to exercise their sick desires. Criminals were treated like victims. The real victims given no recourse through law or by a parliament of fools only interested in creaming off what little wealth remained. Is it any wonder that decent people have had enough?"

At this, the congregation roared. Even Reverend Haigh, watching intently from the wings, clapped and cheered. He didn't seem at all annoyed that Dad's sermon was getting much more approval than his own ever had.

Argyll clapped along with the throng. Only Mum appeared uncomfortable with what was being said and how well it was being received. Sitting the other side of me, Claire looked terrified, like a rabbit in a snare. Her head shot from side to side, her wild eyes desperately searching for an exit. God how I wished we'd left her at home.

"But we cannot stand alone. Scotland cannot stand alone. The porous border is leaking as refugees from the south flee their own civil war. What's left of our military, still loyal to a bankrupt system, struggles in vain to keep order. Indeed, it has formed an alliance with England's military in response to the overwhelming threat on all sides."

Now there were boos. Cries of 'shame on them', 'they should join with us'. Dad motioned for calm. Eventually, he got it.

"Much of this many of you know already. So what chance do we have? What future do we have? Are we doomed?"

An uneasy silence now. It did, indeed, sound utterly hopeless. Dad paused for effect.

"No, I say."

This was greeted with a roar like a wave, starting at the back of the church and surging forward.

"No. Because, when things are at their blackest, that's when the native people of these islands are at their best. History tells us this. Already we have banded together, formed strong local militias to defend our homes, and begun the long process of eradicating those who do not share our ideals. Those whose ideology is alien to ours. Whose beliefs simply don't belong here. Make no mistake, together we can enforce the rule of law and the word of *our* God. Keep our families and our homes safe. And put the British people back in charge of Britain."

Applause resounded around the church, reaching up to the rafters. Dad, looking pleased and relieved, folded away his notes and stepped down from the pulpit. Smith gave him a pat on the shoulder as he resumed his position back at the head of the congregation. While, as Dad marched back down the aisle towards us, he received even more pats on the back from our friends and neighbours.

He took his place back alongside Mum and glanced across at her, looking for some kind of signal, for some kind of acknowledgement. But she couldn't bring herself to look at him and stared down fixedly at her feet.

I watched him though.

I watched him with new eyes.

I watched while his eyes hardened and the need for her approval drained from them. They became glassy, like marbles. He turned away from Mum, his face became fixed, and he stared sternly, resolutely ahead, down the length of the church towards his friend Smith. So what if his wife didn't support him. He had a bigger family now.

"Thanks for that, Alan," said Smith into the pulpit microphone. "Rousing stuff! We'll have to get you into town more often."

Screech!

A sudden high-pitched, ear-piercing, electronic howl filled the church. I shoved my fingers in my ears and winced but it didn't help. Smith, red in the face, was shouting into the little black box attached to the lapel of his uniform. But I couldn't catch it. The feedback subsided but his voice, still raised to combat the vicious electric whine, carried the length of the church.

"What? What? Slow down, man, I can't make out what you're saying…"

Whoever was speaking, whatever they said, it drained the colour from his face.

"They're *where*?" He stopped talking into his lapel and bellowed into the pulpit microphone, desperate for everyone's attention. "Ladies and gentlemen! Quiet please! Everyone, please, listen. I have important news."

It wasn't Smith's appeal that brought the congregation back to order.

It was the sound.

Not more feedback. A different sound.

This was a deep, bass rumble.

It started in your feet and worked its way up into your chest. It made the bones in your face judder. It set your teeth on edge. Made your fillings shake.

The walls of the church started to vibrate. Piles of hymn books toppled. All chatter ceased. The sound grew louder and louder, the vibrations more intense. Smith, meanwhile, had disappeared from the pulpit.

Then, as abruptly as it had begun, the sound stopped.

In our little church a thousand people held their breath.

Then the doors crashed open.

Armed men in uniform marched in, a dozen of them. Some went straight down the aisle and positioned themselves at the front of the church facing the congregation, rifles at the ready, others dispersed to each corner.

Right behind them, an officer and sergeant, recognisable from their insignia. The officer immediately climbed into the pulpit and addressed us. A wail of panic and despair echoed around the chamber.

"Ladies and gentlemen, please remain calm. We are a combined unit of Scottish and English regulars, bound by law to protect you, our citizens. You have absolutely nothing to fear from us."

(I've had plenty of chances to learn since then that, when someone says you have nothing to fear, it's a good idea to get away from them as quickly as possible.)

The officer's words did nothing to calm the people down. There were raised voices, angry fists, distorted faces.

Only Argyll remained stubbornly silent beside me.

And poor Claire. If she had looked frightened before, she was terrified now. Like a cornered animal, her back raised, her neck rigid. She looked around, eyes bulging like the starving corpse-woman I'd first met at the river's edge, desperate for a way out. But there weren't any. Soldiers guarded the church doors, weapons levelled on the assembly. She collapsed into her seat, put her face on her knees and laced her fingers across the back of her head.

Gingerly, I reached out and stroked her hair.

"It's okay, Claire, it's okay."

Empty words.

An empty gesture.

Because the churning in my stomach told me it was anything but okay.

A man's voice raised itself above the clamour.

"If we've nothing to fear, can we leave?"

"Not for the moment," said the officer.

A volley of boos and catcalls. The officer raised his voice over the racket.

"As you may be aware, a new identification system is being introduced throughout the British Isles, replacing the outdated paper passport. Under Directive 1719 of the Council of Allied British States, all citizens are to receive a barcode on the nape of the neck which carries their basic information: name, date of birth, and so on. The system has already been implemented at detention centres and is now being widened to the general population. We are here to execute Directive 1719."

The officer shouted so that the soldiers at the back of the hall could hear. "Sergeant?" One of the soldiers by the door stood to attention. "Bring in the equipment." The soldier darted outside.

In the intervening moments, a hush fell over us. It could have only lasted seconds but felt like hours. At length it was broken when someone asked the question on everyone's lips.

"Why us?" a woman shouted.

The officer looked indifferent. "No special reason. We're working through all the villages in the district in turn. We were just lucky to find so many of you in one place, at one time."

"How long will it take?" asked another.

"No more than a couple of hours... but that depends on how cooperative you are."

This was met, less with distress, than low-level grumbling. The fear of being shot had been replaced by the annoyance of being inconvenienced. This was Easter Sunday after all, and lunchtime was fast approaching.

"It's quite a straightforward process. Simply give us your name, date and place of birth. Your details are checked against our database and, if it all adds up, you're coded and sent on your way. So as not to slow the system down, any discrepancies will be put to one side and dealt with separately. Efficient and simple, which is how we like it."

The sergeant returned with two other soldiers. One carried an electronic tablet, the first piece of computer equipment I'd seen since St Albans. (I was surprised to see computers still existed at all.) The other held a green military carry case in both hands which, from the strained expression on his face, must have weighed a ton. The soldiers started to move down the aisle but the officer stopped them.

"We'll start at the back."

The officer left the pulpit and strode down the aisle to the back of the church. Straight towards us. The soldiers congregated at the end of our pew. The carry case was placed on the floor and the soldier responsible opened it. He took something out that looked like the barcode scanners I'd seen on shopping trips to the supermarket with Mum.

In my previous life.

Four years ago? Or four hundred?

A few hundred miles away? Or a thousand million?

At that moment dread settled on me. I knew we were in trouble but I couldn't work out why.

The sergeant looked at my dad and, with none of the

easy, conversational tone of the officer, barked at him for information.

"Name, date and place of birth." Before adding, almost as an afterthought, "Please."

Dad confidently trotted out the family's cover story.

"Alan Rogers, six, six, eighty-eight. Born in Leicester, England. Now I live with my family at Bridges Farm."

As Dad spoke, the soldier typed what he was saying into the tablet. He stood and waited for a few moments then simply shook his head. The officer turned back to my dad. "I'm sorry, sir, but there appears to be a discrepancy. If you and your family could accompany the sergeant outside."

He gestured towards the open door. Dad looked around the church.

(For who? For what?)

Then he silently led Mum out of the pew and out of the church. Mum looked back over her shoulder at me, her eyes offering anything but an invitation.

Rather than follow them I instinctively reached up and took Argyll's hand. Argyll squeezed it, almost painfully. The sergeant barked his mantra again, this time at Argyll.

"Name, date and place of birth."

"Argyll Roberts. Born nine, ten, seventy-six, Montrose. Current address, the Bridges Farm."

The tablet soldier tapped this in, nodded at the officer, showed him the display. The officer's eyes widened, his curt manner softened and, taking a step back, he gave Argyll a military salute.

"Mr Roberts, sir. You're a war hero, an honour to meet you. And who's this little lady?" He leaned towards me.

"She's my granddaughter."

"Is that right? And where's your daddy, lassie?"

I put on my best and broadest Scottish accent.

"He's dead... of Istanbul."

The soldier with the tablet did his thing, showed the results to the officer. He stood up again and addressed Argyll.

"You and your family have done a great service to your country, Mr Roberts. Your son died a hero at the Battle of Istanbul. May I shake your hand?"

Argyll held out his free hand and allowed the officer to take it.

"There's no record of your son being married, though. It says he was single when he died."

"They were never married because he never came home. This little one's mother died not long after him."

"Mother's name?"

"Ella. Ella Murray."

"Would you happen to know her date of birth?"

"Aye. February sixth, two-thousand-and-two."

Again, the tapping. Again, the nod. The officer, so cold and offhand before, looked almost moved as he read from the screen. "Ella Murray, died in childbirth, March third, twenty-six," the officer's eyes glanced from the screen and on to me. "Survived by her daughter, no name registered. That would be this little one?"

Argyll nodded. I saw that his eyes were shining. I don't think he could have spoken even if he'd wanted to. Instead the officer spoke to me.

"And what name did your granddaddy give you, lassie?"

"Alice," I said.

The officer confirmed this to his colleague with the tablet. "Alice Roberts, born three, three, twenty-six, Elgin. Father William Roberts, mother Ella Murray. Now, if you could step out into the aisle so we can code you, this won't take a moment."

Argyll moved forward into the aisle, leading me by the hand. The soldier placed the barcode reader onto the nape of his neck, flicked a switch and Argyll twitched, grimacing with pain. A series of lines of unequal thickness were left on the back of his neck. They looked red and sore.

Then it was my turn. "It only stings for a second," the officer said. But they all say that.

The soldier lifted my hair out of the way and placed the reader on the nape of my neck. I heard a click, felt a vicious sting, and squeezed Argyll's hand for all I was worth. The stinging subsided and I was done.

"Well done, lassie," the officer said. I felt pleased that I hadn't cried out. Argyll released my hand and stretched his out a few times, then took it back in his bear-like paw again.

"Okay, you two are done, free to go." The officer gestured towards the open door and Argyll made straight for it but I was concerned for Claire and held him back. The officer was trying to get her attention but she was still cowering in her seat.

"Madam? Madam? Can you come forward please?"

I thought I'd make it easier for her.

"This is Claire. She's already been coded."

Claire was rocking back and forth in her seat. The officer gestured and the sergeant moved down the pew and roughly manhandled her out into the aisle. He forced her into a standing position, pulled her hair to one side and displayed the barcode to the officer.

"See?" I yelled. "There's no need to be cruel. She's a refugee."

The officer grabbed hold of the scanner and placed it on Claire's neck. She hissed through gritted teeth. The officer pulled the scanner away and touched it against the screen of the tablet. A moment later the screen lit up and he turned his attention to me.

"This woman is a criminal."

I didn't believe it. I couldn't believe it. The scanner thing must be wrong. "She's my friend. She was starving to death when I found her. She escaped from a refugee camp."

"A refugee?" The officer's voice was scathing. "She escaped from an internment camp. Where criminals are sent."

I was confused. How could it be true?

I looked at Claire. Her eyes weren't pleading anymore.

They were blank.

I stood in shock as the soldiers dragged Claire past me, out of the church. Argyll dragged me out then, too. He was in an awful hurry all of a sudden. I looked back over my shoulder as Claire was stood against a large memorial topped by a stone angel. The soldiers released her and walked away. She collapsed to her knees in the mud so the officer barked an order and one soldier went back, hauled her to her feet, propped her against the cold stone, and retreated. Argyll was dragging me down the path and out of the cemetery but, still, I saw it all. The officer walked up to her, withdrew his pistol, put it to her temple and pulled the trigger. Claire fell like a rag doll.

A moment later, the crack of the pistol shot reached us.

The stone angel looked down at her, implacably, white marble greyed with age, wings disfigured by time. And I remember thinking that at least she wouldn't have far to go to be buried.

(I'd clearly been spending far too much time with my brothers.)

13

Argyll was pulling me down the street, leading me by the hand, but my legs were close to useless and every few steps I stumbled. He didn't get cross with me. Instead, he scooped me up in his arms and ran with me. I looped my arms around his neck and held onto him tightly. His stubble was like iron filings against my soft cheek but I didn't mind it. I was in such deep shock you could have amputated one of my legs and I don't think I'd have felt it.

We ducked down an alley between two cottages and in through the back door of one of them. Smith was in the kitchen, shouting into his walkie-talkie. On the kitchen table was a collection of firearms: shotguns, hunting rifles, pistols. Argyll put me down carefully on a bench seat and I leaned back against the kitchen wall. It was cold, unpapered stone and I was glad of it.

Argyll quickly updated Smith on what had happened at the church, what was still happening. Smith wasn't concerned in the least about the rest of the congregation, only about my mum and dad.

"What did they do with them?"

"They put them in the back of their truck."

As they talked hurriedly to one another, white noise began to growl in my ears.

Insects danced in my eyes.

Then I blacked out.

How long later? I was woken up by Argyll's gentle urging. "Alice? Alice? Here y'are, drink this."

He offered me a cup with some water and I took a few sips. I began to feel better.

Smith hovered behind him, anxious to get going.

"There you go, she's fine. Tuck her in upstairs. I'll leave a note for my wife and she can look after her once church empties out."

"If church empties out."

There was a tension-filled silence that my muddled head struggled to decode.

"I'm not leaving her here alone," Argyll told Smith.

"Well she can't come with us. She can barely stand."

"Then I'll carry her."

"Don't be ridiculous, man. You're going to have your hands full as it is."

I took another sip of water.

"I want to come," I whispered weakly.

Argyll leaned closer to me. "What was that, lassie?"

I tried my voice again. It was stronger this time. "I want to come."

"It's going to be dangerous," Argyll said. "You might see some bad things."

"They won't be the first bad things I've seen," I said.

Smith's tone was dismissive. "Of course, let the ten-year-old girl decide…"

"They're my mum and dad. I want to come," I said with as much finality as I could muster.

I think it was my instinctive understanding of what was going to happen next that made Smith relent, however reluctantly. "Oh, for crying out loud, come on then. Time's a wasting."

Argyll put out his arms, offering to carry me, but I shook my head and clambered down from the bench. Thankfully, my legs held.

Smith shouldered a rifle and picked up a pistol, which remained drawn. He took a quick peek out through the kitchen door. "All clear," he said.

Argyll tucked a gun into his waistband then scooped up the rest of the weapons. "Follow me, stay close, do exactly as I tell you," he said. I nodded and we both trailed Smith out the back door.

14

We were in a village. Which means only one road in and one road out. That's how villages work. Smith had militia stationed at both ends of the village watching every vehicle, and everyone, who came and went.

That's who had warned him while he was in church.

That's why he was able to slip out before the soldiers surrounded it.

That's who we went to meet now.

Men I didn't recognise were hiding behind a stone wall with a clear view of all the activity around the church. Crouching as we went, we crept across an open field and up alongside them. They each took a weapon from Argyll.

"What's the latest, lads?" Smith asked.

"They're letting them out a few at a time," answered a jowly man with a stubbly beard. "It'll take ages to code everyone."

"There's no way they'll do that. They'll want to be off before we get the chance to organise ourselves," said Smith.

"Perhaps we're a bit more organised than they're expecting," the jowly man replied.

The men grinned at one another, grimly.

"Anyone else been held?"

"No, not so far."

"Well done, lads. If they move…" Smith tapped his

walkie-talkie. He gave each of the men a slap on the shoulder as we inched past. A few hundred yards away a small copse offered cover and we made for it. Once safely out of sight we yomped through the undergrowth towards the other end of the village, away from the church. Emerging from the woods, we scrambled up and over a small hill and then climbed a stile into a field dotted with sheep. A second group of militia greeted us here and they exchanged handshakes.

"Who's the girl?" asked one balding militiaman.

"It's his youngest."

The bald man smiled at me and gave me a wink. I said nothing back.

Argyll handed over another rifle and a shotgun, keeping the last one and the pistol for himself.

"We've got back-up coming from the farm," said the bald man. "They're going to meet us there."

"Good. Hopefully we won't need it," said Smith.

We walked off at pace across the field. Everyone except me knew where they were going in advance, all prearranged via walkie-talkie. We emerged at the top of a field that looked down over the narrow country lane and stopped, panting and breathless.

"We're staying here," Argyll said to me as the others trudged down the hill. They took up positions by a five-bar gate at the bottom of the field. I was tired and out of breath, so I offered no argument. If there was going to be trouble, and it looked pretty certain there would be, this was as good a place to watch it from as any.

(I was only ten.)

Below us, Smith and the four patrol members had opened the gate. There was a rusty old car under a tarpaulin abandoned at the edge of the field. They pushed it out into the road while the rest of the militia remained hidden by the hedgerow. They knelt down, facing the road, and pushed the barrels of their rifles and shotguns through the hedge's densely knit bushes and brambles.

Now that I was alone with him, I took the chance to ask Argyll the question that was nagging away inside me. A personal, painful question that I felt intrusive just voicing. But that I had to have the answer to.

"Argyll... what happened to your granddaughter?"

There was a moment of silence that stretched into infinity.

"She died," he replied eventually. I'd figured that out for myself.

"How?" I asked, nervously.

I knew I was prying and couldn't look at him.

Argyll sighed. It was long and deep and sad.

"It was a home birth. There used to be hospitals and midwives and nurses but they're gone now, like everything else. Her mum, my boy's lass... well, there were complications and by the time anyone came to help, it was too late for her. The baby... my granddaughter... she survived a couple of months. Long enough for my wife to fall in love with her. Than the flu took her. I'd not the heart to tell the authorities. They were performing autopsies on flu victims and we didn't want her little body cut up into pieces. So we buried her in the garden, planted flowers over the grave, kept her close by us. But the will to carry on had gone out of my wife. It wasn't long before the flu took her, too."

I realised I was crying. I looked across at Argyll. His eyes shone but he'd had all the tears wrung out of him long ago.

"I'm sorry," I said. I wiped my eyes and nose on the sleeve of my coat.

"Me too."

"That day in the woods. You were following to look after me, weren't you?"

He looked down at me and nodded.

"How long had you been doing that? Following me, I mean."

"Not long. A couple of years. Give or take."

I didn't know what to say. I managed, "Thanks."

"My pleasure, lassie."

I was out of questions and so we sat in silence. But it was a comfortable silence and I was glad that I'd asked him. And that he'd answered.

Glad that the awkwardness I'd felt around him had gone.

Glad that I'd got my Argyll back.

Then, on the road below us, an army truck rumbled into view.

It was closely followed by another.

Smith and the men from the militia took up positions on the far side of the car. The 'captain' had tied a white sheet to a length of pole and waved it from side to side in the air.

Next to me, Argyll stiffened. "Here we go," he said. "Time you were making yourself scarce, lassie."

Not likely.

"I'd rather stay," I said.

He looked down, eyes piercing into me, trying to gauge me.

Was I staying for the thrill?

To gloat?

To bear witness?

Was I strong enough to witness this and everything that came next?

Whatever he read in my eyes, he tore his own away and fixed them back on the scene below.

"Have it your own way," he said.

The lead vehicle in the column slowed as it came around a bend in the narrow road. It screeched to a stop, black, choking clouds of burning rubber spitting from the tyres as it bore down on the roadblock.

The second truck, given a little extra warning, juddered to a halt behind it.

A tractor came rattling up the road behind the army trucks and stopped a few feet away. It was towing a trailer, usually used for transporting bales of hay.

Today the trailer carried men.

Armed militia, each one with a balaclava or knotted hankie to disguise their faces. Two of them seemed familiar, even from where I stood; one was tall and slim with a mess of blond hair, another stockier with close-cropped dark hair.

Tom and Rich.

The army trucks were trapped, sandwiched between the militia.

I couldn't hear anything but, from our vantage point, Argyll and I could watch the whole scene. The officer climbed out of the first truck's cabin while soldiers scrambled from the back, rifles at the ready. The officer exchanged words with Smith, only I was too far away to make out what was being said. Then the officer began to wave his arms more emphatically but Smith just barked back at him. One of the soldiers raised his rifle at Smith and a volley of shots rang out from the hedgerow. The soldiers fell to the ground, out of my sight behind the high hedge, while Smith dropped the white flag and the men behind the roadblock ducked down behind the car. They reappeared holding rifles, which they levelled at the officer.

The officer froze, hand halfway to the pistol at his waist.

While shots were being fired at the first truck, at the rear of the column Tom, Rich and the rest lit rags in milk bottles and launched them at the second vehicle. Two landed on the canvas canopy, two more flew inside the truck's open back. The canopy ignited and soldiers leaped out, a couple of them coated in liquid flame. Their high-pitched screaming reached even my ears as the burning men rolled around on the floor, frantically.

None of the militia stepped forward to help them.

They didn't even put a bullet in them to end their agony.

The rest of the soldiers from the back of the burning truck (there were four of them I think) put their weapons on the ground and knelt down in the road, hands clasped behind their heads. A couple of militiamen stood over them while the rest advanced on the lead truck. Smith moved around the abandoned car, stepped over the dead soldiers and shouted something at the lead army vehicle.

For a few moments, everything was silent.

Everything was still.

Then Mum and Dad climbed down from the back of the truck.

Dad had his arm around Mum's shoulders. She, head down, covered her face with one hand and clung onto Dad with the other.

They were out.

They were safe.

Dad lead her past Smith, stopping to shake his hand as he went by. He took her to the safety of the far side of the roadblock, away from the trucks, away from dead and burning soldiers, to where the men with guns stood. He left her there and returned to Smith's side.

I took this as my cue and ran down the hill towards her.

To my mum.

Argyll yelled for me to stop, then ran after me. There was an 'oof' from behind me and I glanced back over my shoulder to see that he'd fallen heavily on the steep incline.

I ran on, reached the open gate of the field and ran out into the narrow lane.

I came to an immediate stop.

On the road in front of me were dead soldiers, bodies full of holes, lying on the black tarmac in puddles of their own thick, congealing blood.

I felt the air rush out of my lungs and stood in shock, hands on knees, as if winded. All thoughts of going to comfort Mum were dashed from my head.

Dad and Smith faced the lead truck with their backs to me. Smith shouted, "This is your last warning before we start shooting. You don't want to burn like your mates, do you?"

I watched while, slowly, warily, sullenly, the remaining soldiers crept out of the first vehicle. They were immediately disarmed by the group Tom and Rich were part of and then all were lead, hands on heads, armed militiamen at their backs, to Smith and my dad.

The officer, the bodies of his men littering the floor around him, launched into an angry rant.

"You do realise that you're fucked, don't you?"

(This didn't sound like very 'army' language to me but I was to learn better.)

Smith laughed, Dad didn't.

"You attack army vehicles under a flag of truce, kill British soldiers. These are acts of war. And, I barely need to add, treason."

The officer was face to face with Dad and Smith, barking at them with his nose inches from theirs, like one of the drill sergeants Argyll had told me about, bawling out young recruits. He looked from one to the other, tiny bits of spittle flying from his mouth as he yelled.

"While this man," he nodded his head aggressively at Dad, "this man is wanted for harbouring a fugitive, falsifying his identity and possession of forged documents. Oh yes, take it from me, you people are well and truly fucked."

Using the butt of his shotgun, Smith struck the officer full in the face. There was a splintering crack as his nose shattered. He fell onto his hands and knees, blood pouring from his nose and mouth and pooling on the road.

Smith crouched down beside him and said, calmly but loud enough for his men to hear, "Who's fucked now, soldier boy?"

Smith bent and drew the pistol from the holster at the officer's waistband. He levelled it at the back of the officer's head, clocked it, and shot him. Brains and bone fragments joined the smears of blood already pockmarking the road.

The officer slumped to the surface of the road like a puppet with its strings cut.

Or a... scarecrow. Yes, like a scarecrow removed from its supports.

His face was mush but the worst thing, worse even than that, was the hollow, dull sound his skull made as it struck the tarmac. *Thonk.*

I let out a horrified gasp.

It was at this point that Dad turned and saw me. A look of shame flashed across his face. Not, I think, at Smith's brutality. But simply at the fact that I'd witnessed it.

Smith barked an order to the men. His men.

"Take care of the prisoners."

Some, but not all of them, shouted back, "Aye, aye, sir."

Then they hesitated.

"Well, what are you waiting for?" Smith yelled.

And the villagers, farmers, shopkeepers, plumbers, policemen, butchers and brothers laid hands on the soldiers.

Argyll, late on the scene and limping, scooped me up into his arms.

For the second time that day he carried me away.

And, for the second time that day, everything went black.

PART III

1

I am dreaming of the Hanging Tree.

Where Auntie Flick ended her life.

Among its roots, the remains of her tiny, stillborn daughter.

(It's only occurred to me lately that this was the reason she chose to die how she did. To bring herself closer to her dead child. To take her final rest in the cold, bare branches while, not far below, her baby rested among the twisted roots. But I was very young when I found her and, as we get older, our understanding of the meaning behind things gets clearer. Even as they get harder to bear.)

I am dreaming of the Hanging Tree.

I am walking towards it across the dew-wet grass but I leave no imprint in the morning's moisture.

Not this time.

It's as if I'm floating a few inches above the ground. Because I know that if my feet were tied to the earth, I wouldn't take another step. I have no desire to revisit the horror of that morning. But I have become untethered and, despite exerting all my will, all my strength, I am drawn closer and closer.

I keep my eyes cast down, fearful of what awaits them, fearful of the inevitable.

But, inevitably, they are drawn up.

Up.

Up.

The tips of her toes dangle a few inches from my nose.

They are bloated now and purple-grey.

(She's been hanging for a very long time.)

They – the toes I mean – bob up and down ever so slightly as Flick's dead weight tests the strength of her chosen branch.

But she chose it well.

The branch did not break then.

It does not break now.

I look up from the bobbing toes to the bloated feet. Up from the bloated feet to the shit-smeared dress. Up the shit-smeared dress to the rigid hands and stretched-out fingers, the gaps between them almost filled in by the bloating of ages.

(How many years now? Seven? Eight?)

Up the mottled arms to the shattered neck, the ruined rope squeezing out folds of flesh like thick mud between a child's fingers. Up to Flick's rotting face, to the obscenely distended tongue, to the empty sockets where her dancing blue eyes once lived. (Eyes are the first thing the birds go for.)

Her empty eye sockets hold me.

Stare their silent accusation into me.

I tear my own eyes away from where hers had been. And see that Flick's is not the only body gently bobbing in the branches of the Hanging Tree.

Oh no.

If only.

All my nightmares are gathered here.

There is Scarecrow, naked as the day he was slaughtered. His crow-pecked face stares blankly earthward, his head lolls down and his arms are spread wide, wrapped around a sturdy branch like he'd been crucified.

More feet dangle.

More nightmares.

From a higher branch hangs Claire, dressed for an Easter Sunday visit to church. Half of her head is missing thanks to the dead lieutenant's bullet. But she still has one eye left. One eye open. One eye to drill into my soul with.

It makes the same accusation.

I've seen enough and try to turn and run. But the dream holds me in its grip. I am caught like a rabbit in a snare and forced to bear witness, like it or not.

But, unlike a snared rabbit, I can't gnaw off my leg and escape.

My eyes continue upward.

Past the dead lieutenant, only recognisable because of his uniform. His face a hole. The skull a shattered eggshell. How ironic he should find a resting place so close to his own victim.

How appropriate.

Still the dream holds me. Still my wandering eyes betray.

Up still further.

A little higher and there he is.

Nuncle.

The rope is tied so tightly around his neck that even one of my fourteen-year-old hands could close around it. Nuncle's head hangs loosely above, the mouth a fixed grin. He leers down at me, teeth sharpened to points like a cannibal. Like in that other dream of long ago.

(Where is he? Where did he go?)

However, Nuncle's eyes are not blank. They shine with life and widen to acknowledge me. There is no accusation in them.

I start to sob. These others, they are the dead. They are all the pain and violence I have seen and they have a right to haunt me.

(I'm glad they only haunt me at night.)

But to see Nuncle like this? Among them? This is just the dream's way of torturing me.

The dream isn't finished with me yet.

Something forces my eyes to go up further. To the farthest, highest branch capable of taking a corpse's weight.

More than terror waits for me there.

Heartbreak is waiting.

(I feel my gorge rising. Good. Perhaps if I'm sick in my sleep I can wake up.)

Mum is waiting.

Not her, not her, not her. Anyone but her. My mind screams. Perhaps I scream in my sleep. Perhaps I thrash. Perhaps I weep. But it is still not enough to wake me.

She is wearing the dressing gown, heavily patched, that she wears at breakfast. Her arms hang limply at her sides. The rope is tight as a fist around her throat. Her dark hair now mixed with grey hangs rattily and wafts like seaweed in a rock pool as her body gently bobs, bobs, bobs on the leafless bough. Behind this curtain I catch glimpses of her face. Still beautiful. The most beautiful face in the world. The face of all my mornings and evenings. The first thing I see when I wake up, radiating love like the sun. The last thing I see at night, giving off comfort and warmth and safety.

The face of a dead thing.

Still beautiful, a fresh kill not yet devoured by time or weather or rot. Still clearly her. Still definitely my mum. (Even in the darkness of a nightmare, my mind could not conjure a picture of my mother in agony.) Her face frozen. Lifeless. Still.

And then her branch snaps.

And she plummets down. Towards my upturned face. Filling my field of vision.

Not her, not her, not her.

Not Mum.

"Sshhh, sshhh, it's okay, Alice. It's okay."

There is a voice whispering in my ear. A gentle hand running through my hair.

"Sshhh, sshhh, there, there, sweetheart."

My thrashing and screaming has woken Maggie. She has climbed into bed beside me. Her arms are wrapped around me, cradling my head. Her body is pressed against mine, warm and gentle.

"It's okay, Alice, it's okay, it's only a dream."

Maggie's gentle urging pulls me out of it. Back towards the surface. I weep in her arms, muttering nonsense and then softly, gently, drift back to sleep.

This time, thank God, it is dreamless.

2

Maggie joined us at the farm after losing her gran in a flu epidemic the previous winter. It took half the village with it so that there were now barely enough souls left to make it worth opening the church on a Sunday. Not that we bothered with that sort of thing very much these days.

For Dad, too much of a risk.

For me, too many bad memories.

During the outbreak we'd been quarantined at the farm and by the time Dad ventured back to the village, the very old and the very young were nowhere to be seen. Not above ground anyway. But there were fresh graves in the cemetery and no one with the will or spirit left to mark them with headstones.

More broken hearts with no one to heal them.

Next thing we knew Smith pitched up at the farm one morning, shotgun over his shoulder, two militiamen for company, and Maggie at his side. Mum and I were finishing up in the kitchen, Dad was upstairs and God knows what the boys were up to. Smith didn't knock, just let himself in at the kitchen door.

"Can I have a word with your husband Mrs, um, Rogers?" he asked, stamping the mud from his boots onto Mum's freshly mopped floor.

It was raining hard and the walk from the village had taken its toll on Maggie. Her hair was plastered to her face, mud had splattered her coat and the hem of her dress and her shoes were caked in it. She carried a small, battered suitcase and this, too, was worse for wear. She looked almost as messy as I did most of the time and, knowing how neat and tidy her gran always kept her, my heart went out to her.

Mum stood wiping her hands on her apron. "Hi, Maggie, lovely to see you," she said warmly. "Alice, can you go and find your father please?"

I soon returned with Dad. Smith had made himself at home at the kitchen table. Still wearing her muddy clothes, Maggie stood awkwardly at his side while Smith's pretend soldiers were at ease either side of the kitchen door. Mum had furnished everyone with a cup of what passed for tea these days.

"Brian, good to see you," said Dad, pumping Smith's hand and I thought (and in contrast to Mum) genuinely pleased to see him.

"I know, Alan, it's been a while, what with the epidemic and everything."

"What can I do for you?" Dad sat down, nodded towards Mum, a signal to equip him with tea (nettle? mint?) too.

Smith put a paw on Maggie's shoulder and drew her closer. "You may have heard, young Maggie here lost her gran in the epidemic. What with the other losses in the village, there aren't many who can take her in. I thought of you."

Dad leant back in his seat, folded his arms across his chest. Mum had abandoned the washing up and had turned to face us, leaning against the kitchen sink, very much engaged.

"We'd like to help but we're a bit hard pressed."

"Of course we can take her," Mum cut in. "We'd love to have you here, Maggie."

"The crops haven't done well. The livestock's been decimated," Dad continued assertively, talking over her.

Mum tutted loudly and turned back to the washing up.

(I don't know what it must feel like to be twelve years old and have no one, to be bartered over, to be passed from hand to hand and have your future hanging from a thread. I hope none of you have known it. My family had its problems, God knows, but at least I still had one. Back then.)

Smith cut in. "We like to think we're a community around here. That we help each other out when there's trouble. Maggie comes from one of the oldest families in the village. And we, the local community that is, have been very accommodating even to people who are complete newcomers. Favours must be paid for." I certainly understood what Smith was getting at, so I'm that sure Dad did.

"I think the debt has been repaid many times over by now, hasn't it Brian?" he said. "We've both shed blood and spilt it."

It was quite startling to me to hear Dad answer Smith back like that. Smith was the militia commander, the man who had rescued Mum and Dad from the army, had killed to free them. For the most part, from what I'd seen, when Dad was with Smith he did as he was told. This, then, was something new. But Smith was older now. He didn't go anywhere without his bodyguards these days which, looking back, is a clear sign of weakness. And the light of certainty had gone from his eyes.

My dad had bodyguards of his own to call on if required, I suppose. Tom and Rich were both built like barn doors and with five years or more militia experience under their belts. Never mind the constant drilling and training Argyll subjected them to. If it came down to a battle of wills, if there were a disagreement or falling out, Dad knew he could call on loyal and committed support. And if it became a battle of wits? Well, my money would definitely be on Dad.

"We've no milk since the goat died. We've no meat since the pigs died. Our old sow isn't likely to give us another litter any time soon. And we've had so much trouble from disease, from vermin and from poachers that we barely have enough chickens left for eggs. God knows we don't taste meat from one month to the next."

Dad painted a pretty stark picture. I hadn't heard our situation set out quite that bleakly before. Mum must have known the reality which is, I suppose, why she backed down that quickly.

"So excuse me if I don't exactly jump for joy at the prospect of taking in waifs and strays."

I wouldn't be put off so easily.

I liked Maggie.

She'd always been nice to me. I hated to see her like this, looking as if she wanted the floor to open up and swallow her, rain dripping from her hair and everything she owned packed into one shabby old suitcase.

"But, Dad, she can help us with the planting. And the harvest," I chirped in.

Dad turned his gaze onto me, ungrateful for the interruption and for questioning his authority.

"And Mum's always going on at me to help in the house more, with the cooking and cleaning and everything. Maggie would be brilliant at that. Which would give me more time to lay snares and go scavenging, the things I'm good at."

Mum had turned back to face us, eyes shining.

"You do have the space. A spare bedroom," Smith blustered.

Thing was, we didn't. The room Claire had used during her time with us was now Dad's. He and Mum hadn't shared a room for ages. A cruel silence settled on the kitchen. Neither of my parents wanted to talk about this, least of all in front of Smith.

"Please, don't put her in the spare room. She'd be lonely. Maggie, I'd love to have you in with me." I walked over and took the suitcase from her. "Now take your coat off and sit down." She smiled shyly and let me help her out of the muddy coat.

So now I shared my room with Maggie and, for the first time since St Albans, I had an actual, real girl friend.

(I discount cannibals that I'd mistakenly saved from starvation. They really aren't best-friend material.)

We'd both lost people we loved so that, while I wasn't an orphan like her, I knew how she must feel about losing her gran. I didn't probe, I didn't pry, I just let her be sad when she needed to be and inched my way forward when I thought the time was right.

We were very different, of course. Maggie was pretty and prim and neat while I always looked as if I'd crawled through a hedge backwards. Which, on some days, I quite literally had. She was better at the domestic stuff – cooking, cleaning, mending clothes – than me because I was all fingers and thumbs but she struggled with the heavier fieldwork. And, even with the self-defence classes Argyll gave us all, she wouldn't have been my first choice of companion when shit went down.

(Sorry for the language. Much to Mum's annoyance, being around Argyll had done nothing for my sense of decorum.)

An extra bed was put in alongside my own and at nights, after lights out, before sleep took us, we would chat together and giggle. About books we'd read, the latest happenings on the farm, how much we loved the dogs, dreams we had of escaping together when we were older.

Freakishly, Maggie also had a thing for Rich. Yes, that one. My bone-headed, knuckle-dragging brother. She thought that she was being subtle but to me it was clear as the tolling of the church bell. Somehow, she would always bring the conversation around to him and no matter how many embarrassing stories I told her, it didn't seem to put her off.

(When it comes to boys, there's just no accounting for taste.)

It was nice to have her there when the nightmares came. They were getting more regular the older I got. Even as the rational part of my sleeping brain told me there was nothing to fear, not really, and that I'd soon wake up and it would be gone, the irrational side was throwing horror after horror after horror at me. At times like those, a comforting word and a cuddle from Maggie were always the best medicine.

But there are, unfortunately, some nightmares you can't wake up from.

Because you're not sleeping.

Because you're dreadfully, terribly, awfully awake.

These are the nightmares people create for themselves.

And they are the worst nightmares of all.

3

It was getting harder and harder to find enough food.

Dad hadn't been exaggerating when he talked to Smith. Things at the farm were bad. Our scavenging trips were taking us further and further away from home. We knew it was dangerous but we had no choice. There were gangs of displaced roaming the countryside who were far hungrier than us and we'd heard enough stories (and had had quite enough personal experience, thank you) to know that it wasn't just the wildlife that they would satisfy their appetite with.

Desperate times breed monsters.

The animals on the farm had suffered as much as we had over the last few years. We'd lost them to disease, old age and simple bad luck. We limped from month to month, season to season, with meat on the menu only if we were lucky with the fishing lines or snares. Although I seem to remember, as a special treat, we'd killed a chicken at Christmas that had had to go around seven of us.

Winter storms had levelled half the orchard. (But not the Hanging Tree. Oh no. That would survive a hurricane, I'm sure. Just to taunt me.) Thank God that the potatoes hadn't been blighted as they helped stave off starvation during the worst of it. But, unless we were happy with a wormy apple for lunch and a mouldy baked spud for dinner, the family diet was going to need a little more variety.

Really, we should have been grateful.

God knows we were better off than many hundreds of thousands, perhaps even millions, of other people. But gratitude won't fill a hungry belly and we weren't about to sit around complaining when we had Scotland's larder on our doorstep.

We'd cut back some of the woodland around the farm to give us firewood for the winters and more growing land. (We didn't dare cut down too much or we risked exposing the farmhouse to unwelcome eyes.) Even the small inroads we made had affected the amount of game I was catching in my snares. We'd disturbed the rabbits' habitat and their numbers had dwindled. Or they'd just gotten smarter and run off. While the amount of pheasants (not the brightest of birds, pretty much bred to be sitting ducks) had gone down to nothing.

Which left squirrel, a very stringy substitute for rabbit or game.

As a result, scouring the countryside for anything and everything edible had become part of the family routine. At first Mum was against me going but I kicked up such a fuss that she had no choice. Initially there was mickey-taking from Tom and Rich but they soon shut up when they saw how fit I was, outpacing them over short and long distances. How good at tracking I was, able to spot and follow sign that their eyes simply passed over. And how good at trapping I was.

Argyll had taught me well. Given me special attention. Mum and Dad were, I'm sure, relieved that Argyll watched over me and, more to the point, had equipped me with the skills to survive the dangers of the disintegrating world outside. In his mind, I wasn't a substitute granddaughter, I *was* his granddaughter. Certainly, that's what the code on the back of my neck said.

For Tom and Rich this was an opportunity to tease me that was simply too good to miss.

"Are you sure you're still part of our family?" asked Tom.

"Yeah, the code on your neck says you're related to Argyll, not us. We should disown you, put you out on the road and let you fend for yourself," said Rich, backing Tom up as usual.

"I'd cope much better on my own than you two would."

That shut them up. Because they knew it was true.

Little sister: one. Big brothers: zero.

At first, our scavenging trips had been super successful. We brought back rabbit, hare, a pig, even the odd sheep. We fished the rivers and came back with fresh catch for dinner. We ransacked abandoned fields and farmhouses, turned up tinned food, dry goods, crops that hadn't been harvested, bringing home sacks of carrots, turnips, swede, all excellent additions to the menu. All a great help in keeping the famished wolf from our door and pawing at someone else's.

But the thing about clearing out an abandoned farm is, you can only do it once. Because cupboards, cellars and storerooms don't refill themselves.

Kitchen gardens don't replant themselves.

Fields don't resow themselves.

More and more often now, we came back with very little to show for our trips away from home.

But at least we did come home.

"We're going south again," Tom told me as I strode out of the kitchen after breakfast (porridge oats and water – I think they used to call it 'gruel'), knife at my waist, backpack with emergency rations strapped firmly in place. "We've not gone that way for a while, might get lucky."

As I stepped outside I whistled for the dogs. They came bounding out of their kennel, tongues lolling, hot breath steaming in the icy morning air. They rubbed up against my legs and I patted their flanks. I'd seen them grow from puppies into fine, strong, animals. Half-wild, half-tame, totally loyal. With them at my side, I felt invincible.

"Morning, Blackie, morning, Vi. Sleep well?"

"No time for play, not if we want to be back for dinner," Tom said sternly, as usual under the false impression that, because he was older than me, he was my boss.

"There won't be any dinner unless we get lucky," observed Rich, not inaccurately.

Argyll met us at the bottom of the field. He'd already been checking snares in the woods.

"Any joy?" I asked, falling in beside him.

He shook his head. The canvas goodie bag over his shoulder hung limply, empty once again. "Perhaps we'll have better luck out in the wild."

"Or worse."

Nice one, Rich. He looked at our annoyed faces and added, "I'm only saying what you're all thinking."

It had been a misty morning up by the farmhouse and the mist got denser as we descended down the bottom field, across the rickety gangway that bridged the stream, and out beyond the edge of what we considered home.

"Stay close, Alice," Tom said, all serious. "Don't get lost in the mist. Dad would have my bollocks."

I felt a surge of anger redden my face and nearly told him where he could shove it. He wanted to sound all grown up and know-it-all but I wasn't some little girl, I was nearly fifteen and had been patrolling the area around my home for years. Get lost in the mist? I could walk it with my eyes closed and not so much as get my feet wet in the puddles.

Ironic. As it turned out.

The further we went, the foggier it got. When we'd crossed the stream I could still see Tom and Rich ahead of me but now they were indistinct shapes, little more than outlines. Blackie and Vi loved it though. They ran here, there and everywhere, panting heavily, disappearing first to my left, then the right.

I remember thinking, *what's the point if you can't see anything?* I mean, how are you supposed to find food or hunt game if you can't even see your hand in front of your face?

Argyll must have reached the same conclusion at exactly the same moment. "This is pointless," he grumbled. The grumbling dislodged something at the back of his throat and he was shaken by a coughing fit. He hacked and hacked, hands on knees, and spat a ball of phlegm into the dirt.

"Pointless and dangerous," added Tom. Stating the obvious had become a big thing for him. "Easy to get lost in this."

We stopped walking and drew closer together. "Let's head back," said Argyll.

We all accepted the inevitable.

"Mouldy spuds for dinner again tonight," said Rich, miserably.

"Better than most people get. You should be thankful, boy." Argyll always had a way of getting to the point.

"Don't call me boy. Old man." Rich snapped back.

Oh, this was a cheery new development. Fighting among ourselves. Hunger makes the best of us snappy. If you're already prone to snappiness it makes you even snappier.

"Okay, okay. We're all disappointed. Let's just head home." For all that Tom's self-appointed leader routine could be annoying, he did have a way of heading off trouble before it got started. "Alice, where have Blackie and Vi got to?"

I shouted into the fog for them and they circled back towards me. They seemed excited. Their senses heightened. They both panted heavily and sniffed the air, nostrils twitching, heads alert. "Come on, stay close," I said. I crouched down and held them by the skin of their necks. They pulled against my hold, eager to tear off into the fog again.

Spooked? Or a scent in their nostrils?

I thought I knew all their reactions by now but this time I couldn't be sure.

They pawed at the dirt, whimpering.

"You know, if you can't control them..." Tom said.

"Of course I can control them," I shot back at him.

"Clearly," said Rich.

They tore free of my grip. Off into the fog.

And I ran after them. By myself.

Unthinking. Stupid. Childish.

"Blackie!" I yelled. "Vi!"

By the time I'd come to my senses I was alone.

And I was lost.

4

Fog has a way of deadening everything.

My voice got swallowed up by the thick air. My desperate cries for the dogs fell flat. Failed to carry.

The warm white breath pumped out of me like a steam engine, became one with the fog. Perhaps that's what fog is, I thought. The breath of a million mouths, trapped by dawn's chill and held there.

Every time I heard a yelp (or thought I did) I changed direction and raced towards it. While the calls from my brothers and Argyll (they couldn't be that far away, could they?) were random.

Distant.

Directionless voices coming out of the mist, deadened by the dead air.

I stopped running as soon as I realised my mistake. Realised how disorientated and alone I was. Now I stumbled on blindly with one arm stretched out in front of me.

The fog couldn't go on forever could it?

It would lift as the sun rose higher and warmed the air. That's how fog works.

But, 'til then, what was the best thing to do? To carry on stumbling around and risk turning my ankle, dropping into a ditch or falling into a stream?

Or to stay in one place and wait until someone found me?

But what if the someone who found me wasn't someone I wanted to be found by?

Ahead of me, emerging from the mist as I fumbled forward, the branches of a small tree. At about head height. Their elaborate symmetry getting clearer, more solid as I got closer. Twin branches suspended in the milky air.

(Where was the trunk? Of the tree, I mean.)

A triangle took shape between the branches.

(Funny looking tree trunk.)

And then the triangle nodded.

And snorted.

I froze on the spot. My heart hammered in my chest like a snared rabbit pounding its hindquarters, frantically trying to free itself.

But this wasn't fear I was feeling. This was excitement. Pure, palpable excitement.

I held my breath and inched forward, extending an arm out in front of me, palm up.

Guiding me on.

Towards the stag.

Emerging from the fog with every step I took forward.

Erect.

Proud.

Magnificent.

Like something I'd conjured from a dream.

(One of the good dreams that is, not one of my oh too common nightmares.)

He raised a foreleg and pounded at the earth. Shook his mighty head.

The antlers cut little ribbon trails in the fog.

By now I was close enough to hear him snort.

Would he bolt?

Would he charge?

If he did, he'd flatten me.

I didn't care. I carried on inching towards him, my hand raised to touch.

I looked straight at him, into the horizontal pupils, arranged to give him nearly 270 degrees of vision. He can look to the front, to the side and almost all the way around without even moving his head.

(Imagine that. Imagine how useful that would be.)

If you want to sneak up on a stag, you have to sneak up from behind – and risk getting your skull caved in with a kick from his mighty hindquarters. But I wasn't sneaking. I was walking straight towards him. His brown-black eyes stared straight back into mine.

His massive lungs pumped warm steam into the fog-filled air.

(Can a human heart burst with pure excitement?)

And then gently, trembling, he let me put my hand on his nose.

I felt the moisture of the fleshy nostrils. The warmth pumping through the dew-wet pelt. The power surging within him.

I stroked his face.

Up and down.

Once.

Twice.

He moved his head down slightly, towards me, inviting my touch.

Surely I was dreaming? What stag, freeborn king of mountain and glen, crowned with horns of glory, lets me, a little lost girl, pet him?

I think I might even have cried a little bit.

I shushed him as you'd shush a horse. Stroked his neck and then, with confidence growing, worked my hands along his side. Down towards the flanks. Feeling his life thrill under my fingers. The heat of his body through the pelt. His mighty ribcage working up and down, tons of muscle effortlessly moving his massive skeleton.

And then my fingers stopped.

Sprang back.

Frozen in the tiny space between his flesh and the chill air.

I stood statue still, barely daring to breathe.

His flanks had been torn open.

That's why.

That's why he had let me touch him.

That's why he hadn't fled.

Deep ragged lines ran along his side, scything cuts through skin and muscle that went deep into his flesh. Holes oozing blood. Offering slow, tormented death.

Claw marks.

What could have done this?

For an insane moment I thought, perhaps Blackie and Vi. That would explain their nervous excitement, their agitation. The smell of a king stag on the air. But this was a beast well beyond them. Chasing frightened rabbits down a hole was one thing. But one well-aimed kick from him and, well, they wouldn't recover, let's put it that way. All their claws were good for was ruining your favourite jumper and not a lot else.

As I said, an insane thought.

What did that leave?

And then I realised that we – the stag and I – were not alone.

5

I couldn't see it but I could sense something behind me.

I span around.

Movement in the mist.

The fog being displaced by...

What?

Something growled. Low and angry. Like a dog only deeper, more primal. More evil.

It lurked at the edge of visibility. Pacing up and down. Sniffing the air and pawing at the earth. I took a step backwards, into the stag's flank. He flinched but held his ground. Unconsciously, I raised a hand to his shoulder, protectively. As if *I* could protect *him*.

"I won't let it hurt you again," I said.

Human arrogance in the face of nature's savagery, sharpened by hunger and ages of time. Now I knew how the frightened rabbit felt in its snare. As my hammering heart reminded me with every beat.

The shape divided into two. And the two halves ranged about in the mist. Dark, indistinct, patient.

My fogged senses cleared. There were two of them.

Of course there were.

Whatever it was didn't hunt alone.

It certainly wouldn't hunt a fully grown stag by itself. Not with the risk of being gored to death or kicked into next winter.

Then the third one came for me.

It flew out of the fog to my right. Like an arrow. While I'd been distracted by the two in front of me it had advanced, inch by silent inch, on padded feet armed with six-inch claws.

The wolf leapt.

Its teeth sank into the flesh of my right shoulder. Its weight crushed me down into the mud. Winded, I don't think I did more than grunt. Then I caught my breath and screamed. Screamed and screamed and screamed. As the wolf, digging its teeth into my shoulder up to the gums, threw me around like a toy. Like I'd seen Blackie and Vi do, so many times, with their much smaller prey.

Agony is just a word. It's impossible to describe true agony, real pain. Only people who have experienced something similar can come close to understanding. And most of them are dead. Just the fact that I'm able to tell you this story means that I did not die but whenever I think about the attack.

The agony.

The memory of the pain comes back. Along with wave after wave of nausea.

The wolf shook and shook its head, burying its teeth deeper and deeper into the muscle and sinew where shoulder meets neck. My face is half-buried in the mud and I'm struggling to breathe, feel as if I'm drowning and being torn apart at the same time.

Behind me, I'm somehow aware that the other two wolves have moved in on their kill. Have leapt onto the flanks of the wounded stag to continue what they'd started. The injured stag, already weakened by his awful wounds, bucks and kicks, turns circles to shake them loose. But the damage has already been done and his slow, brutal death is only a matter of time.

I was an electric circle of pain. Every nerve ending in my body was convulsing, retching. I had enough clarity to think, *this is how I die.*

Then, through the fog, despite the agony, I heard a familiar noise. Higher-pitched than these beasts. Far more welcome. The barking of dogs.

My dogs.

Blackie and Vi, my guardians since childhood, raced into the circle of Hell I was being savaged in and set on my attacker. But ten thousand years of taming had reduced their claws and teeth to mere ornaments compared with the wolves'. The one on me didn't so much as flinch or lessen its grip. The two on the stag leapt from his sides and onto Blackie and Vi. There was a blur of blood and fur, teeth and claws, as the four animals wrestled in the dirt. Barks, yelps, whimpers, growls.

Vi tore off into the fog. Her attacker followed. Blackie lay on his side panting, his muzzle smeared with blood and saliva. One wolf stood astride him, a giant paw crushing his face. It sunk its teeth into Blackie's neck. His hind legs kicked out obscenely as the wolf pulled back its head and, with it, a chunk of meat and fur.

I closed my eyes.

So this is how it ends.

My last moments spent watching my brave, beautiful dogs die in even greater agony than me.

Then, gunfire.

Not a shotgun's blast – a sound I knew well.

Not a pistol's crack.

But a gunshot. High calibre. Close enough to register even through the wall of pain I'd retreated into.

Another shot.

Then a third.

The beast's head stopped shaking. The wolf's jaws stopped

working. Its teeth stopped gnawing. Its grip on my soul loosened and I felt its dead weight collapse onto me.

I lay panting, bleeding in the mud. Waiting for life to leave me.

The one eye that wasn't buried in the dirt looked out into the fog and saw a man appear out of it. He knelt in the mud beside me. Pulled the dead beast off me. And cradled my head in his hands.

I felt the warm blood running down my neck and soaking into my clothes and I knew that I was dying. And then I knew I must be dead because the man turned into an angel.

And the angel had Nuncle's face.

6

In my fevered dreams they all came to visit me.

Nuncle.

Flick.

Claire.

Even Scarecrow. Stalker of my childhood nightmares.

"Is this Heaven or Hell?" I asked him.

What if it's neither?

"Am I dead or aren't I?"

What do you think?

"Stop answering me with questions."

Stop asking questions you already know the answer to.

"I'm not dead then?"

If you were dead, you'd know whether there was a Heaven or Hell already and wouldn't need to ask.

"Then I'm dreaming?"

And fighting. Even as you dream.

We were both silent. Then he asked me, *Do you want to know? Or do you want to keep fighting?*

"Do I want to know what?"

The answer to the question everyone has asked since people first got smart enough to ask it: what happens when we die?

I considered this for a moment. Maybe two.

"I think I can wait to find that out."

I felt him smile even though, as a creature without lips, it was impossible for him.

Then keep fighting.

7

The first face I saw when I woke was Mum's. For weeks I'd fought and sweated and, in my delirium, screamed blue bloody murder, and she hadn't left my side. She'd held my hand all day. Had slept in Maggie's bed each night. Mopped up after me when I soiled myself. Cleaned and dressed the weeping wounds in my shoulder.

"Alice, Alice, mummy's here."

Her voice penetrated my dulled senses and I opened my eyes. It was sunny outside and the room was bathed in light. Or perhaps it came from her.

"Mum," I croaked.

She smiled. A weary smile. She didn't smile very often in those days so any smile was welcome. "Someone else is here to see you."

Mum gestured down to her right and Vi's head popped up beside my bed. Excited, I tried to sit up but stopped short as a pain like a branding iron shot through my shoulder.

"Easy, easy," Mum said and, leaning over, helped me into a sitting position, pushing pillows behind my back to prop me up. "Vi's been keeping us both company, haven't you, girl." Mum absently stroked Vi's head. I couldn't move my left arm to nuzzle her; it was bound and held in place with a sling. Vi lifted her forepaws onto the bed and rested her head on them. She whimpered, missing Blackie, I could tell.

"I'm sorry, Vi. Mum, they killed Blackie."

I couldn't help it, I started to cry. Which set Mum off, too.

"We know. We know all about it."

"How can you? Is Uncle Nick really back or did I dream it?"

"Uncle Nick's back," she answered, unable to suppress the excitement in her voice. I hadn't seen her so excited in years. Since, well... since Nuncle had left and our lives here had started to unravel. She went on, almost babbling. "It's been two weeks and I can still hardly believe it. It... it's a miracle. I'd given him up for dead years ago. He had to be shoved out of your bedroom most evenings."

Her hands were trembling. She managed to contain herself and went on, more calmly now. "Even Tom and Rich got all weepy about you. Rich was so angry I thought he'd do himself an injury. And Argyll! Oh my word. He's been poorly too so we've had to keep him away in case you catch his cough. But he says he'll never let you leave the farm again, not without a rope attached to his wrist and an armed escort."

That sounded about right.

"Maggie's been helping me clean and dress you. She's only not here cos she's doing my shift in the kitchen. And, yes, your dad too of course. He's got a lot on his mind but he's been very concerned."

"Please, Mum, tell me what's been happening. Tell me about Nuncle."

"Not yet, dear. I don't think you're ready."

I gave her my most persuasive, pleading look. But it cut no ice. I'd have to work harder on it.

"Hon, this is the longest you've been awake since the attack. It's the first words you've said in weeks. You need rest, not excitement. Now, go back to sleep."

She leaned over and started to stroke my hair. Like she had when I was little and couldn't sleep or had been woken by a nightmare.

I closed my eyes, went back to sleep and, for the first time in a long time, dreamed a dreamless sleep.

9

I woke to find Nuncle waiting for me.

He'd saved my life twice on that nightmare day.

The first time from the wolves.

The second time from the wounds.

My wolf (which I know is a funny way to think about it, but that's just how it is) was an adult female hunting with two young adult males. Probably her own pups. When a wolf attacks, it goes for the throat. It knows that this is a weak point, with muscle, sinew and blood vessels that aren't protected by bone like elsewhere in your body. And if it can get a grip of your windpipe, you don't have a prayer. Thank God she never sank her teeth in there. Or into the big veins and arteries either side.

Once Nuncle's bullet had shattered her spine…

(I'm not even kidding. After two warning shots, when the wolf didn't let go and he was close enough, he killed her at the first time of asking. But the part about how he learned to shoot is coming up next so I won't spoil it now.)

The biggest risk to me was from blood loss and infection. By acting quickly and putting on a field dressing right away, Nuncle saved me from both these dangers and saved my arm at the same time. (Which I would have rather died than lose anyway.)

"Morning, munchkin, how're you doing?" he asked.

"Nuncle."

It felt strange to say this name out loud after so many years. It must have felt strange for him to hear it, too.

"No one's called me that in a century," he said, smiling. The smile played around the edges of his mouth but it didn't reach his eyes. Wherever he'd been, he'd seen too much for his eyes to smile very easily.

I did my best to talk to him like the old Nuncle. The Nuncle I used to know. The Nuncle that I'd loved. "Eight years isn't exactly a century now, is it," I teased.

"It's most of your life. You've changed. A lot."

"So have you." It was true as well. It wasn't just his eyes that gave him away. He'd aged. He must have been forty-something but looked much older, more like sixty. Grey in his hair and stubble, hollow cheeks, sunken eyes, exhausted. But there was still enough of my Nuncle in there for my heart to feel lighter just for seeing him.

"I thought I must be dead. When I saw you, I mean."

"I thought you were going to die."

"Did you know it was me?"

"Not right away. I saw the wolves attacking and knew I had to do something. I was just glad I didn't hit you by accident. I'm a good shot but in all that fog, it could have happened. At first I thought you were a boy but, once Tom and Rich found us, I put two and two together and realised it had to be you."

"Eight years is a long time, isn't it."

"A very long time."

"You must have been surprised when you saw Tom and Rich."

"No shit."

I opened my eyes wide in mock shock horror.

"Sorry," he said.

"No need, I've heard a lot worse. You've met Argyll by now?"

A smirk. There he was, the real Nuncle, poking out from behind his old man's mask. "I couldn't believe it when I saw the pair of them. Tom's a foot taller than me. And Rich's built like a brick..." he collected himself, "...wall."

"And me?"

"Well, you grew up beautiful. The image of your mum."

It was nice to hear. A comfortable silence settled over us. But I had too much to ask, there was too much I needed to know, so I had to break it. "Where've you been?" My voice had an edge that I couldn't quite hide.

"Everywhere," he answered quietly.

That wouldn't do. Not at all.

"Where did you go first, after you left us?"

"Your mum says that I'm not to tire you out and it's a long story."

"Listening isn't tiring. Anyway, I need to know or I won't be able to sleep."

"Okay then. But it will have to be the short version. I can fill you in on the details when you're up and about again. Deal?"

"Deal."

(It was lucky I got him to talk to me then. I never did get more details from him.)

"First I drove south. Back across the border to England. But the further south I went, the rougher things got." He laughed at the irony. "A walk in the park compared to how it is now, I suppose. But still tough. There were roadblocks all over the place and the petrol soon ran out, so I abandoned the van and carried on on foot. I kept my head down, kept drifting south, kept out of people's way. Slept rough, scavenged what I could off the land. But it was getting harder and harder to find food. Too many other people were getting the same idea. So I signed up."

"To what?"

"The Army, munchkin. The 'regulars' as you call them around here."

This surprised me. Nuncle had never been a fighter. "What did they do with you?"

"First off, I was sent to the Middle East. It's a very hot, dry place. It's sand, mostly. A sea of sand. In every direction, stretching from horizon to horizon."

I found it hard to imagine. Growing up in Scotland had left me with hardly any memory of 'hot', 'dry' or 'sand'.

"Why were you sent there?"

"I was a fireman." He saw my face register surprise. "No, not the kind you're thinking of, munchkin. Someone who saves cats stuck up trees or puts out house fires. Army firemen put out fires in the oil fields. You see, some people didn't want the oil to be sold to us anymore. So they blew up the oil fields and the flames burnt and burnt, so black and thick that the smoke blocked out the sun. Firemen went into the oil fields and put the fires out."

"It sounds super dangerous."

"It was. But, well, we were pulled out in the end. They needed men for the war. The real war. The last war, I suppose. So I trained for combat."

"Is that where you learned to shoot?"

"Yeah. It turns out I have a gift. A steady hand and a sharp eye. I became a sniper. That's someone who crouches out of sight, often high up, with a good view of the area around them, and he uses his rifle to pick off enemy soldiers, one by one. Often they're very far away. And often, they don't know what's hit them until they're already dead. That's how I learned to use the rifle I shot the wolves with."

I think my jaw must have been hanging open because Nuncle smiled, leaned forward and ruffled my hair.

"Where were you a sniper?"

"I was at Istanbul. A huge battle that lasted for years. Men came from all over the world to die there. All the sides in the war were fighting one another, making alliances then breaking them, betraying each other. You didn't know from one day to the next who was on your side and who wasn't. It was a great big, bloody, awful mess."

Istanbul. That rang a bell. It was where Argyll's son had been killed.

"Argyll's son died in that battle," I said.

"Did he? The old guy hasn't really said that much to me."

"He was in the army for years himself before that."

"Sounds like a useful man to know these days."

"He's more than a friend. I got coded," I leaned forward and showed him the tattoo on the back of my neck, "and pretended to be his granddaughter to confuse the soldiers."

"I got coded too," said Nuncle, turning his head to reveal the marks. "But mine says exactly who I am."

"Did we win?" I asked.

Nuncle looked confused. "Did we win what?"

"Istanbul. Did we win?"

"Nobody did. In the end, when all the bullets had been fired, when all the missiles had been launched, when all the sides had lost enough and killed enough, everyone went home. No winners, only losers."

This sounded awful and completely unlike all the wars that I'd heard of or read about. Where, in the end, the British Army always won because they deserved to.

"And then you came home?"

"Yes. A lot of us turned around one day and headed back to England. There was no official retreat, no surrender, so there was no transport. But we picked up our things and left."

"A long way?"

He smiled, "Yes, a very long way. It took me two years to get back."

"Two years?" My voice pitched up in surprise.

"Yes, munchkin, two whole years. Istanbul is in Turkey, right across the other side of Europe. I had to walk a lot of the way. Getting the odd ride. Catching the odd boat. But a lot of walking in between. And a lot of fighting, too."

"Did you kill a lot of people?" I asked, genuinely curious. I wanted to get an idea of what time and war had done to him.

To the Nuncle I'd known when I was little.

The Nuncle who wouldn't have hurt a fly.

"Yes," he answered, his voice thick with regret. "Lots."

A gloomy silence descended.

"You must have been happy to get home," I said, trying to lift the mood.

"Oh yes. Overjoyed."

His eyes said the opposite.

"What was it like? After so long?"

"Things had been bad before but they'd got much worse. Most of the Army had been posted abroad and what was left behind had lost control. Gangs had taken over the streets, there was no law, no order. People fought for food or they starved. If you weren't prepared to fight, you were as good as dead."

"So you decided to come back to us?" I asked hopefully.

"That's right, munchkin. Nowhere else much to go and so… here I am."

Nowhere else to go? Were we the last resort? That stung. I buttoned my lip and didn't make a big deal of it. I suppose it was as he said. He'd been away from family for years and that would change anyone.

"So how did you find us all in that fog?"

"Oh, the wolves left a very easy trail for me," he went on.

"But a sniper rifle's no good in the fog, so there was no point in tracking them for the sake of it. Then I heard the shouts and screams and just came running. When I saw the attack I knew I had to shoot, fog or no fog."

"I was lucky you didn't shoot me, too."

"Kinda lucky. But you weren't moving much by the time I got there. You. Or the wolf."

"But what were wolves doing there in the first place? Scotland doesn't have wolves."

"It does now," he answered.

He could see by my eyes that this was not a good enough answer.

"Oh, there'd been talk of reintroducing wolves to Scotland for years to 'manage' the wildlife."

I must have looked sufficiently blank for him to add more.

"Some people thought that there were too many deer, that they were threatening the natural balance because there were no predators to keep their numbers in check. It's possible for them to starve too, you know."

"So?"

"So there was talk of reintroducing wolves to the Highlands to cull the deer."

"But this isn't the Highlands."

"I know. Hunger must have driven them south. Private landowners had introduced wolves onto their own lands. Clearly, when everything broke down, the wolves got loose. There's nothing a predator likes more than chaos."

"So the wolves were brought back deliberately to kill the deer?"

"Pretty much, yeah."

"But deer are beautiful."

"There's only so much beauty allowed in the world before someone will decide it's time to start killing it."

"And the stag? He was the most beautiful thing I've ever seen. Did he die?"

"He was as good as dead when you found him."

Tears stung my eyes. Why, I don't know. Of course the stag was dead. What a stupid thing to ask.

"He didn't die for nothing, munchkin. He's helped to keep you alive, all this time."

"What do you mean?"

"There's enough meat on a fully grown stag to feed a family for an entire winter. You don't just leave that to rot in a field. We went back, me, your dad, Argyll and the boys, and butchered him where he lay. Carried the cuts home. There was so much meat we couldn't carry it all, took two trips. And you've been eating him ever since, we all have. Your mum has fed you broth, soups, stews. What an injured person needs more than anything, apart from rest, is to get their strength back. Well, that stag has shared his strength with you. He kept you alive when death was hanging on your shoulder. His strength is in you now."

A calm settled on me then. I could have been disgusted at the idea of being fed by the dead stag. How were we better than the wolves, if that's how we lived? But, instead, learning this had an entirely different effect on me. I felt a sense of rightness. Like having the stag inside me kept him alive in some weird way.

"Don't you think you earned it, Alice?"

"What do you mean?"

"You stood alone to defend a dying animal from a pack of wolves because he was injured, because he was beautiful. I've been at war for the last eight years and the bravest thing I've ever heard of is my own niece defending a dying stag from a wolf pack. Have you any idea how daft that is? Crazy brave." He leaned over and planted a kiss on my forehead. "Just don't do anything like that ever again, understand me? Ever."

His eyes locked on mine. I managed a weak nod.

"Anyway, I've already talked your head off. Get some more rest. With any luck you'll be well enough to get up in a couple of days. Sleep well, munchkin."

He stood up off my bed, retreated from the room and quietly closed the door behind him.

I didn't get to sleep for hours.

10

A few days later I was well enough to make my first excursion downstairs, gingerly taking one step at a time while clinging to the bannister with my good hand. I sat at a chair in the kitchen while Mum and Maggie busied themselves with domestic chores.

Despite their small talk – or because of it – I soon got bored.

I was itching to go outside. Walk the perimeter of the farm and outbuildings. Check on Vi, feel some air on my cheeks.

"Mum, can I go outside?"

"Not yet, dear, you're not strong enough."

Then, ten minutes later, "Mum, can I go outside?"

"No, I've already told you, you're not strong enough."

After an hour of this, she was ready to kick me outside.

"I won't go far," I said as I wriggled into my coat. She looked back at me with resignation in her eyes.

Out of that stifling kitchen at last, the clean air of the highlands hit me straight between the eyes. I drank it in. Cutting back the trees had opened up a new horizon and, on a clear day, you could see for miles. The view was simply beautiful.

It was hard to believe anything bad had ever happened here.

It bore none of the scars.

They were something only people carried. Inside and out.

If we were to disappear overnight, nature would restore itself in no time.

Trees would regrow.

Fields would become havens for wildflowers.

Moss and ivy would take over the farmhouse and work their slow magic, rotting wood and grinding stone into dust. A few years and there'd be hardly a trace of us left. Hardly anything to say we'd ever even been here.

Nature would be better off without us, that's for sure.

I started a slow circuit of the farm, clomping in oversized boots. I kept being told I'd grow into them but suspected that I'd already done all my growing. Two pairs of thick socks kept them from rubbing but, more than anything, I craved an item of footwear that hadn't been broken in by feet other than my own and fitted me like it was meant to.

Just once in my life.

Wouldn't that be nice?

I heard clanking and banging, metal on metal, coming from one of the barns and hobbled towards it. It was only a few yards away but the effort was incredible. I was panting for breath in no time, my forehead beaded with sweat, and I could feel icky moisture oozing down my back. (Yuck.) And it wasn't even my legs that were injured. I began to realise just how poorly I'd been, how touch and go surviving the wolf attack had been. How many weeks ago now? Three? Four? And still barely able to put one foot in front of the other.

I reached the barn and stuck my head through the open door.

Inside, Nuncle and Dad.

It was so bizarre to see them together, occupying the same space like that, that it struck me with almost physical force.

More than half my lifetime had passed since I'd last seen them together. I stood and watched silently, catching my breath, while they busied themselves.

The old camper van that had brought us up here had been left in the barn under a big tarpaulin since the petrol ran out, oh, ages ago. Now the covering had been peeled of, the bonnet was open and so were all the doors, front, side and back. Nuncle was leaning over the engine, hands fiddling with something inside. Dad was across the other side of the barn, kneeling down in front of a row of old oil cans, systematically picking them up and shaking them.

One made a sploshing sound. His face lit up and he stood, quickly at first then stretching out the small of his back, as rusty as the can he was holding.

He turned to tell Nuncle what he'd found. "Hey, Nick, bingo."

As he turned he saw me watching shyly from the doorway. He looked at me curiously. "Well would you believe it. What do we have here? A young lady."

My hair had been left to grow out while I was recovering so I suppose I did look a bit more ladylike than the tomboy who'd been wolf bait. Now I felt even shyer. Around my dad, too.

Weird.

Nuncle looked up from the engine and turned towards me. He beamed.

"Alice. Up and about at last."

"Mum agreed to let you out?" said Dad. "Clearly we can add 'wolf attack' to the list of things that do nothing to diminish your powers of persuasion."

I wondered whether he was cross – it was sometimes hard to tell with Dad. Then he smiled and I knew I wasn't in trouble.

"What are you doing?" I asked.

"Oh, nothing much," said Nuncle, wiping his hands on an old rag.

"Just seeing if the old camper van has any life left in her," added Dad. "While you've been out of action, your uncle Nick has been proving very handy."

Nuncle looked a bit sheepish.

"He's added all kinds of new skills to his repertoire since we saw him last."

Dad walked across the barn and put an arm around Nuncle's shoulders.

"He helped me fix the wind turbine which, while not exactly cranking out the megawatts, means we can run the freezer again. And that's perfect because we have a half hundred weight of venison to see us through the winter and we don't want it going off."

Dad sounded almost bubbly, light-hearted. Like some of the weight had been lifted. And not, I understood right away, just because our food worries had been put to bed for a few months.

He'd missed Nuncle too.

Of course he had.

He'd known him an awful lot longer than I had.

And whatever had happened to drive Nuncle from us had been a long time ago now.

My dad's little brother was alive. My dad's little brother was safe. He'd come home to us. Of course Dad was happy.

"Can you fix it?" I asked Nuncle.

"Oh, I wouldn't have thought so. The electrics are completely buggered," said Nuncle dismissively.

"But," added Dad, "if we can get the engine running, we could put it in the old tractor – which is well and truly buggered – and then replough the field come the spring. Which will set us up for the whole of next year." Dad suddenly realised how boyishly optimistic he was sounding and reigned it in. "At least, it gives us a fighting chance," he added.

"How are you, munchkin? Shouldn't you still be in bed?" asked Nuncle.

"I had to get out and stretch my legs, couldn't stand it any longer. Where are the boys? And Vi?"

"They're all off with Argyll and the militia," explained Dad. "Not too far from home this time. After the near miss with you, we're going to keep the excursions to a minimum for a while."

I suddenly felt a little faint. "I think I need to go back to the house now," I said.

"Do you need a hand?" asked Nuncle.

"No, I need the exercise. I'll take it slow. See you later."

"See you later," said Dad. He went back to rooting among the rusty cans.

"See you later, Alice," said Nuncle.

I turned and slowly inched my way back to the house. I'd overdone it. Maggie had to help me back up the stairs and put me to bed.

But I extracted a promise from her to let Vi up to see me when she came back from patrol. And told her to plead with Mum to move back in with me. "I'm clearly much better and you can help me get dressed and stuff, cos with one arm out of action, I'm pretty much useless."

So that night, for the first time in ages, I slept with Vi at the foot of my bed and my best friend snoring beside me. (Did I mention Maggie was a snorer? Neat and pretty when she was awake but sounded like a litter of piglets when she was asleep.)

I stared at the wall opposite my bed. The Snow White wallpaper had faded. The white a dirty yellow, the dwarfs just smudges, the paper peeling at the edges and bulging where the damp plaster behind was causing it to distort.

Nuncle had papered that wall. A surprise for me when I

first came here, to make my new bedroom feel less scary, more like home.

But from the moment he'd left it had never felt homely.

And now that he was back, I could only hope we would be whole again.

A family again.

11

A couple of weeks later I was feeling much stronger. My walks around the farm had become that – walks – rather than feverish stumbles. I could do laps of the entire perimeter without feeling ill from it, Vi constantly at my side, skipping ahead of me, boundless in her energy and love. She was certainly helping me to build up my stamina.

Even my sore arm was beginning to loosen up. The muscles had withered while it was in a sling so I made it my mission to strengthen it, at first using pebbles as weights and curling them like I'd seen my brothers do, working up to bigger and bigger stones from the walls around the farm.

Injury or no injury, wolf attack or no wolf attack, I wasn't going to fall into the trap of becoming a weak little girl. Regular goading from Tom and Rich, who seemed to have got over their guilt for losing me that day, would help see to that.

"Hey look, it's Alice," Tom would say.

"Don't worry about her, she's armless," Rich would answer.

And then they'd laugh themselves even stupider at how funny they were.

(Big brothers. God love them. Annoying as Hell but what I wouldn't give to have them here with me.)

I also had a goal, which always helps when you're trying to get better. I wanted to be well enough to walk to the village on Christmas Eve. The carol service was pretty much the only family outing that was left to us.

(Church going isn't a high priority for families on the verge of starvation. Neither were trips away from the safety of the farm when the countryside is overrun with the desperate and the destitute.)

Everyone in the district made the effort at Christmas. The village church, even with holes in the roof and broken windows, took on a whole new character when lit with candles and torches. While people in the decimated congregation, who used to see each other weekly and now didn't one month to the next, took great heart from catching up with each other and sharing their news, however bad it might be.

Plus, this year was different.

This year was super special because our family was whole again. This year, nothing was going to keep me away.

Christmas Eve came and me, Mum and Maggie toiled in the kitchen making a big batch of venison stew to take with us to the village as a Christmas offering. Dad thought that we were mad, wasting good meat, but Mum was adamant.

"I've not seen a procession of people coming out from the village to help us," he observed.

"There are people who won't have tasted meat since last Christmas," she argued. "We got lucky. It almost cost us our daughter's life but we got lucky. We have enough to see us through winter. Who else around here can say that? If we can't share our bit of luck at Christmas then there's no hope for us. We don't deserve to survive."

She was adamant. Dad stormed off while we busily cut the mould from spuds, carrots and parsnips that, a couple of years earlier, would have gone to the pigs, and tossed them into the largest cooking pot we had. After a couple of hours on the stove, though, it began to smell delicious. It even drew a crowd, with Tom and Rich all of a sudden very interested in hanging around the kitchen.

"When's this getting served up?" asked Rich.

"You two, clear off," Mum told them. "It's not for you. I'm putting some aside for our Christmas meal tomorrow but we're taking the rest to church this evening. And I'll be leaving a guard on the pot to stop either of you stealing any."

They loped off looking far from happy.

We made quite the procession along the old trail into the village. The path was more overgrown as we used it less, but still passable. It was already pitch dark, of course, and a frost had formed over the puddles which made the way less muddy. Dad and Nuncle lead with a lit torch each, firearms slung over the opposite shoulder. Mum and Maggie followed, carrying the cooking pot between them as my arm still wasn't up to it. Tom and Rich brought up the rear. Poor Argyll had ruled himself out of making the trip and taken to his bed again, the cold weather having brought back his persistent cough with a vengeance. Even so, I felt a cheery glow about me having the family all together like this.

"What about a carol?" I said. "While we walk." Walking behind me, my brothers snorted their derision.

"We're not the von Trapps," Dad replied, failing entirely to enter into the spirit of things.

"Come on, Dad. A Christmas song. Warm up our voices for the carol service."

"Yeah," said Nuncle. "Don't be such a miserable sod, Adam. A song will make the walk go faster."

"And let every starving cutthroat for miles know that there's a family of idiots walking around in the dark with a big pot of venison stew singing Christmas songs."

"Adam, we're carrying lit torches," said Mum. "If there's anyone who wants to cause trouble, they already know we're here, song or no song. What were you thinking of, Alice?" She turned to ask me.

"Oh, I don't know, it was just an idea." All the controversy had made me feel shy. I was regretting mentioning it in the first place.

"My gran always liked 'O Little Town of Bethlehem'. She used to belt that out at Christmas," said Maggie.

"Let's give that one a go then," chimed in Rich from the back, suspiciously supportive all of a sudden.

"Okay, on three," said Mum. "One, two, three."

We began a tremulous version of 'O Little Town'. Quietly at first but building in confidence and volume as everyone joined in, even Dad. At least until the end of the first verse when, one by one, we realised that those were the only words we knew and each of us dropped out. Except for Maggie. Her clear, sweet voice carried on through each of the verses, carrying the song by herself all the way to 'Our Lord Emmanuel'. Then she stopped in her tracks and started to sob.

Her and Mum put down the pot. Mum threw her arms around Maggie's shoulders.

"I just miss her," she said, her face buried in Mum's chest.

"I know, hon, I know. But we're your family now, aren't we?" Mum looked around the rest of us for support.

"Of course we are," I added and joined Mum in wrapping my good arm around Maggie. Mum looked up and motioned to Tom and Rich. They came and joined in, throwing their bear-like arms over the top of ours. Then Nuncle and finally, reluctantly, even Dad.

"There, you see," said Mum looking down at Maggie. "You've got all of us now. And we aren't going anywhere, are we?"

Maggie's sobs subsided and she managed a weak smile.

"Now, come on," said Mum, wiping away Maggie's tears.

"Let's get to church and warm them up with some of this stew. It's exactly what your gran would have done if she were still here."

Maggie nodded and, bending, picked up her handle of the cooking pot. Mum took up the other side and we resumed the slow procession.

Lights through the trees in the distance let us know that we were nearly there. However bleak a year it had been, the village had still come out to do its best on Christmas Eve. There was no electricity anymore, of course, but as we drew closer we could see lights twinkling inside the old church, illuminating the stained-glass windows. Despite the cold and the hunger and the sheer, bloody awful that we lived with day to day, it did look quite homely. Christmassy. And I felt the old warmth rise inside me.

We entered via the ruined lychgate and walked up the path through the cemetery. Only one tree stood in the churchyard now, the rest cut down for firewood and to clear more space for the dead. There were a lot more graves than I remembered.

New graves.

Mounds of mud that would never get a headstone.

No one left to cut one.

No one left to engrave one.

Those kinds of things are luxuries when every single day is a struggle just to stay alive.

We were greeted by a sentry at the door, one of Smith's militia. He looked barely any older than me. Ridiculously, he stepped forward, levelled a shotgun at us and actually used the phrase, "Who goes there?"

Behind me, Tom and Rich spat out a laugh.

"You can bloody well see who it is, Barry," said Dad. "We're carrying bloody torches. Now get out of the way and let us in."

"Err, yeah, sorry. Smith's orders," he stammered, standing to one side to let us by. He looked thoroughly miserable.

"Is that thing even loaded?" Dad asked. Barry shook his head.

"Dickhead," Rich said to him as we filed past.

At least the church still had its doors. Enough – what, faith? Hope? Respect? – remained that they hadn't been stripped for firewood. The hinges creaked as Nuncle shouldered his way through so that the small congregation all turned as one to look.

A sea of ghosts.

White faces. Hollow cheeks. Sunken eyes.

The old had all been taken but even the young who had so far avoided disease, starvation and death had become prematurely old.

Faces lined with want and worry.

The pews that had been regularly packed, now mostly empty. Little clusters of frightened people dotted around the place. Denuded family groups. A congregation once united by friendship, now divided by suspicion.

But the church itself. Well, they'd done what they could to make it welcoming. The lights we'd seen from outside were candles placed on the window ledges and they made the place feel warm and welcoming. They flickered in the drafts created by the missing panes in the stained-glass windows so that a dancing sea of shadows played constantly across the walls. Some moth-eaten, old decorations had been dug out from somewhere and dotted about the place. Fake holly wreaths, angels and stars, you know the kind of thing.

If I'd still been six I would have thought it was wonderful.

But where was she now?

In that moment I envied her, my six-year-old self. To still believe in everything, still see through those unpolluted eyes. To have no clue what the future might hold.

There's a lot to be said for not growing up.

Now, Smith saw us and stood to greet us. "Adam, great to see you. Nice of you to make the effort." I'd not seen him since he'd dropped Maggie with us, what, nine months earlier, and time had not been kind. My dad and the boys had caught up with him often, of course, for their remaining militia duties, patrols and stuff. But they never bothered to tell me how he was or anything. I really didn't like him, never had, so I never asked.

But I was shocked.

If he'd been showing signs of wear and tear nine months earlier, he looked on his last legs now. He swayed as he stood. Seemed to have shrunk inside his clothes. Dad hurriedly strode down the church's centre aisle, hand outstretched, as if he wanted to save Smith from the embarrassment of collapsing.

"Good to see you, too." Dad shook his hand vigorously. "The whole family's here."

"I see that. Tom, Rich." Smith nodded in their direction and they in his. "And little brother, the prodigal, returned. I heard you were back, Nick. And you've been busy learning new skills. We'll have to talk about some militia duties for you, we could do with some recruits."

Smith extended a hand and Nick took it. But he seemed in no hurry to take Smith up on his offer of being roped into the militia.

And that was it as far as introductions went. It seemed that only the men of the family were worth acknowledging in Smith's eyes.

"We had to leave Argyll behind, his chest's no better and he wasn't up to the walk," Dad explained.

"Oh, Argyll's a tough old bird," said Smith. "A bit of bed rest, he'll be up in time to toast the New Year. Like a good Scotsman. Give him my best."

Mum stepped in. "We are actually quite worried about him. We wondered whether Dr Barnes was here?" She craned her neck, looking around the meagre congregation. "Hoped he might come out to the farm to check on him. After Christmas Day, of course."

"Barnes is no longer with us, I'm afraid," said Smith.

"Really. Where did he go?" asked Mum.

"The same place as everyone else." Smith rolled his eyes upward, heavenward. "You look after enough people who are dying, you wind up dying yourself. Typhoid. Last spring. Not even a grave. He diagnosed himself, knew it was hopeless. Told us to burn down the surgery with him in it so there was less chance of it spreading."

"My God, that's awful," said Mum.

"We removed the last of the medicines, what little there were, before we torched the place. I even gave it a kickstart with a wee bit of petrol that I'd put by. Oh, he had a grand send off. Up in ashes, like a Viking chieftain."

He said all this with real relish. It was as if he was enjoying himself.

I wondered if Smith had lost more than weight.

He also seemed to have lost his mind.

"We've had to take care of our own since the good doctor departed. Anyway, not to worry. It will be me next, I'm sure. Or this old bugger." Smith motioned toward Rev. Haigh who had been sat beside him in the front row. Haigh was dozing, wrapped up against the cold under layers of clothing.

Smith aimed a kick at him. "Hey, wake up, Haighie. We have guests."

Haigh opened his eyes and squinted at us, first trying to get us in focus and then to remember who we were. "Ah, the Rogers. Welcome, welcome." He rearranged himself into a more upright position.

"Happy Christmas, Vicar," said Mum. "We've brought a little supper with us. To share with the congregation. I think there'll be enough to go around."

"Very generous of you, Mrs Rogers. Very generous. Can I...?"

Mum and Maggie put down the cauldron on the top step leading to the pulpit and Mum lifted the lid. A delicious smell drifted out. Smith and Haigh peered in.

"Stew?"

"There's meat in it. Venison," Maggie said.

"We got lucky. Alice's dog caught the scent of a calf and we managed to trap it. Just a small thing but we wanted to share our good luck," said Dad, clearly keen not to let on that we had a freezer full of meat back at the farm.

Generosity was one thing.

Stupidity another entirely.

The prospect of something warm to eat sparked the people into life. Haigh sent a couple of them off to the manse to gather plates, bowls and cutlery and an orderly queue formed down the aisle of the church. Mum had brought a serving spoon with her and was soon dishing out dollops of stew to the ragged congregation. Everyone sat together in the first few rows to eat and soon there was chatter where there had been silence. Given there were only thirty or so it went around everyone easily and a queue for seconds quickly formed.

While these were being wolfed down, I saw Nuncle whisper something to Mum and then slip away from the church. I'd wondered whether this might be too much for him. I'd been a bit surprised when he decided to come along in the first place instead of staying behind to keep an eye on Argyll. "Getting away from his damn coughing for a few hours will do me good," he'd explained. "Plus, if there's any trouble..."

But I wasn't surprised that he was making an early exit.

Too many people.

Too many memories.

And only bad ones.

Haigh laboriously climbed up to his pulpit to address the congregation. "First of all, thanks to the Rogers for coming today. They certainly brought some Christmas cheer, didn't they? That's the best meal I've had in six months."

Murmurs of agreement and a chorus of 'thank yous' from the villagers.

"We don't have many reasons to be thankful these days, do we?" Haigh went on. "But we've survived another year and we're still here to tell the tale. So let's try a carol shall we? Page 174 in your hymn books. 'Oh Little Town of Bethlehem'. One of my favourites."

A mumbled, quavering version of the song began. We glanced along the line at one another, shared a family smirk. There was no music but we added to the atmosphere by belting it out. Some of the congregation shifted in their seats, turned their heads in our direction. It was their turn to think someone had lost their minds, I think. But we'd already had a dress rehearsal. And Maggie's eyes shone.

There were a couple more carols, a Lord's Prayer, and then Haigh wound things up. He offered Smith the chance to come up and say a few words but Smith declined.

A sign of his own decline, I think.

Refusing the chance to take centre stage?

To hear the sound of his own voice?

He was broken now and I felt no sympathy.

The people started drifting away, back to their cold stone houses. And we set off back to the farm. No sign of Nuncle, so Tom joined Dad with the torches at the front of our little procession. I helped Mum with the cooking pot now that it was empty and easier to carry. While Maggie followed behind with Rich, chatting together and occasionally giggling.

Did we feel better for our visit? Did we feel lighter? I know I did. There was a lot less tension between us on the walk home. Even Dad, so sullen these days... months... years... chatted easily with Tom. Just doing something normal, like something from our old lives, lifted the weight we bore a little bit and, for the first time in a long time, I felt happy.

12

Argyll hung on until Boxing Day.

So I was glad that I spent some time with him the day before.

He was too poorly to come downstairs for the Christmas meal and I took a bowl of the venison stew up for him.

He was dozing and I whispered him awake. "Argyll… Argyll…"

I moved the bowl around under his nose to see whether or not that would help. His nostrils twitched a little and his eyes fluttered open. "What's this, sweet girl?"

"A bowl of Mum's stew. It's good. You won't get better if you don't eat."

"Help me up."

I put down the bowl on his bedside table and helped him as he struggled upright. The movement brought on a coughing fit. It went rattling through his body, making him curl in on himself. He shook with it and brought mucus up onto the bedclothes. There were specks of blood in it. Some of the mucus clung to his chin in a thick, yellow trail. I'd brought a tea towel upstairs with me to rest the bowl on and I used this to scoop up the mess, quickly as I could, to save him from embarrassment.

The coughing seemed to last forever. Every blast of it caused me to wince. Eventually it subsided to a hollow wheezing and his body uncurled again. He leaned back into the nest of pillows behind him, slowly, like someone getting into a bath that's full of too-hot water.

I took the glass from his bedside table and held it to his mouth. He had a few sips and I wiped the drips away. He cleared his throat. "Thanks, sweetheart. Let's give this stew a go."

I held the bowl up under his chin and spooned in a mouthful. He chewed slowly, turning it around and around his mouth. He was so thin that I could see every muscle and sinew working under his paper-thin skin. With an effort, he swallowed. And then it caught and he started coughing again. Not so bad this time and a mouthful of water saw it on its way.

We tried another mouthful.

And a third.

Then he shook his head.

"That will have to do for now, Alice," he said, exhausted from the simple effort of eating. "You leave the bowl there and I'll try some more later. Go back to the family now."

"Okay, Argyll. Merry Christmas."

"Merry Christmas, Alice." He managed a weak smile and closed his eyes.

That night he had a coughing fit that woke us all up. I was two rooms away but I lay there listening.

It was only bronchitis wasn't it?

He would get better wouldn't he?

Once the weather got warmer and not so damp.

At breakfast, Nuncle looked dog-tired. "I suppose you all heard that coughing last night? I mean, I gave him some water and propped him up but I might have to move into the lounge, sleep on the sofa or something. I don't know how much more I can stand."

"Should I go up and see him?" I asked Mum.

"No, let him rest," she answered.

In the end it was Maggie who found him. Mum sent her up with a cup of tea a couple of hours later while the rest of us were out and about doing our chores. They knew I would be the saddest as I'd been closest to him so they waited until I came back in for lunch. Mum and Maggie were sitting together at the dining table looking serious and I knew immediately something was up.

"What's the matter?"

"Sit down, love. It's about Argyll."

The rest of what she told me just sort of blended into the background. I didn't run around the house screaming or tearing my hair out. I just put my head down and cried to myself quietly. While, inside, another little bit of my heart broke.

"Can I go and see him?"

"If you like, love. We've tidied him up."

It was a funny thing to say. But what would the right thing be?

As I learned afterwards, when Mum felt I was ready to hear the details, Argyll had haemorrhaged, most likely after the coughing fit that had disturbed us all the night before. Sometime between Nuncle getting up and Maggie taking him tea, he'd brought up a lot of blood, more than his weakened system could afford to lose, and his heart had given out.

That was, as best she could work out, how it had ended for him. While I was outside that morning, they'd done what they could to make him presentable, washed the blood from his face, changed his clothes and the bedding, as they knew that I'd want to see him as soon as I was told.

And that was how I found him.

Thin sticks under a thin, white sheet.

Head resting on a clean, white pillow.

His pale, drawn face still as a mask.

I'd seen death before, of course I had, when I was younger and more frightened. For all that I liked Auntie Flick and had made a friend of Claire, Argyll was the first person who I really thought of as family that I'd lost.

(He wouldn't be the last.)

And because of this, it struck me differently.

Not with horror. But with deep, deep sadness.

He'd filled a gap left by absent grandparents.

He'd filled a gap left by Nuncle.

He'd filled the gap my dad couldn't fill because of how my dad was.

And he had watched over me when there was no one else to.

If you could ask most people how they would choose to die, they'd answer at home, in bed, close to the ones they loved. In that sense, he was lucky, wasn't he? As I was to have had the chance to say goodbye.

(God knows, that's rare in the world these days.)

Thing is, I don't really believe he would have chosen to go that way. Weakened. Eaten away from inside. Not when he had always been strong and active and sure. I think he would have wanted to go quickly, doing something worthy. Laying down his life for a cause. Like his son had. To have had a death that meant something.

His arms were outside the sheet and I reached out and put my hand on top of his. Cold. I already knew it would be. I left my warm hand on top of his cold one, hoping to transfer some of my warmth into him. To leave some trace of myself with him and draw some trace of him into me.

Then, for a long time, I sat on the edge of his bed and wept.

Eventually, as the day that never really got light ground its way around to dusk, Mum sent Maggie to check on me. She perched next to me on the bed, took my other hand and sat with me for a few minutes. When I had no tears left in me she led me by the hand back downstairs to the kitchen. Everyone was there now.

"How you doin', munchkin?" asked Nuncle.

I managed to mumble an, "Okay."

"Eat something, love, that will make you feel better." Mum put a hot drink and some warm food in front of me. I picked at it. "Not hungry," I muttered.

"We need to talk about the funeral," said Dad, ever practical, ever cold.

"Give us a minute," Mum pleaded.

"What I wanna know is, who's gonna be on hole-digging duty?" said Tom around a mouthful of bread. "That was always Argyll's job."

I flew across the table at him.

Clawed. Scratched. Pulled. Bit.

I would have clawed out his eyes if I could have.

Even with my bad arm, it took three of them to peel me off him.

13

The fag end of a long winter.

My shoulder much better.

The pain of Argyll's death subsiding into memory.

Days spent grubbing for food.

Evenings spent huddled together trying to keep warm.

Lots of early nights.

All silently praying for spring. Kinder weather. Softer ground to dig and plant in. Animals coming out of their winter places to scrounge for food that we might catch to feed ourselves.

The winter stag had seen us through the worst of it but only just. The cupboards were almost bare, the chest freezer under lock and key in the cellar only a few cuts away from empty.

Tension mounting. Parental silences. Arguments carried out in angry whispers.

Then, one night, a creak in the corridor outside my room.

The single creak of a floorboard and I was instantly wide awake.

I sat up, winced as a stab of pain bit my shoulder, but was recovered enough by now to swing my legs over the side of the bed and lever myself upright.

If I hadn't got out of bed that night, if I'd ignored that creak, laid where I was, everything would be completely different now. My curiosity cost the lives of the people I love most. I know that. And I carry the guilt of it with me every day. A vivid, raw, red scar that divides the present and the past. Getting out of bed that night set in motion a chain of cause and effect that I'll have to live with forever. I only wish that I had the chance to rewind my life and undo all that was done.

But life doesn't offer us those chances.

Maggie, who in contrast to me slept like a log, was snoring away as usual. I thought better of disturbing her, crept around her bed and tiptoed to the door.

Perhaps I'd imagined the creak?

No, there it was again.

Another.

Definite this time. Who would be sneaking around the house in the middle of the night? Unless it was one of the boys looking to pilfer food from downstairs.

I bet that was it.

I took the doorknob and turned it, gently, silently as I could, opened the door a crack, peeked through. Holding my breath, I drew the door in towards me and leaned out into the pitch blackness of the corridor.

Just in time to see Nuncle disappear into Mum's room and ease the door closed behind him.

I shut my bedroom door as silently as I'd opened it and crept back to bed.

Why?

What could be so urgent that it couldn't wait until morning?

It was a while later when I heard another creak. Footsteps going back the other way. No need to leap out of bed this time to check whose they might be.

In between and afterwards I lay awake staring at the cracks in the ceiling.

Staring a hole into it.

Until late winter's weak light stole in across the room. Maggie snuffled, then stirred. And the house grudgingly roused itself to life.

14

After that first time I kept a vigil.

Deliberately kept myself awake as long as I could in case there was a repeat.

I'd drink a lot of water before bed so that my sleep would be disrupted by the need to pee, which would help me wake up and to stay awake afterwards.

What was I thinking?

Did I even have a plan?

I think I thought that I would creep out and say 'Hi'. Just ask Nuncle what he was doing. I was curious, that was all. Curious what it might mean.

(Beyond the obvious, of course. I wasn't a child anymore. I was fourteen and grew up on a farm, so I knew all about *that*.)

Trying not to sleep at night was making mornings tricky. I yawned through breakfast and dragged my feet through my chores.

"What's the matter with you, sleepy-chops?" asked Rich, ruffling my hair.

"Oh, it's my shoulder. It still aches, keeps me awake at night," I lied. A convincing one, though, that even got me sympathy.

As I kept up my vigil night after night, the hole I'd thought in the bedroom ceiling got bigger and bigger.

Until, one night, I had it.

It hit me like a lightning bolt.

Suddenly, I knew.

Was so sure that staying awake wasn't a struggle anymore. I ached for dawn to arrive so that I could talk to her about it. It had to be her, Mum I mean, not Nuncle.

I'd have to be smart. To get her alone. And it had to be tomorrow.

15

After breakfast the routine was that Maggie would stay with Mum and help her tidy up in the kitchen. Tom and Rich would go with Dad to do some heavy lifting, chop wood, clear fields, fix walls and farm buildings, that kind of stuff.

Nuncle went along too but tended to go off and do his own thing, sometimes take his rifle and go hunting.

Then we'd all circle back to the kitchen around lunchtime to get warm and to eat whatever Mum and Maggie had been able to conjure up for lunch.

Before my arm, I would go with them and then disappear into the woods to check my snares. Since my arm, though, I was on light duties. Not strong enough to carry heavy stuff and Mum still too scared to let me wander beyond the edge of the farm. I'd take some kitchen scraps for the old sow and watch her gobble them up. Collect the eggs from our scrawny chickens. Gather some wormy, windfall fruit from the floor of the orchard, stuff like that.

But this morning, I wanted Mum to myself.

My arm story had set me up nicely when I asked Maggie if she'd feed the pig. "Of course, Alice. You rest up here, stay warm. I'll take the kitchen scraps." She threw on her coat and breezed out with the plastic bucket.

"See if there's any fruit, too," I said as she went out. I didn't want her coming back too soon.

I waited a few minutes, sat at the kitchen table and watched Mum labouring over the kitchen sink. How many years had she done this for now? Kept it all together? Dragged us all through this?

If Dad was the head of the family, she was its heart.

"You okay, Alice?" she asked, busy drying the dishes. "Think you're up to putting some of these away?"

I was nervous, didn't know how to bring it up.

What if I was wrong?

It certainly wasn't impossible.

She might think I'd gone mad.

I went over to the sink and picked up a pile of clean plates, took them over to the sideboard where they lived. I turned around and her back was to me, leaning over the sink again.

What if Maggie came back? It had to be now.

"Mum?" I said.

"Yes, love?"

"Take me with you."

She paused for, what, a heartbeat, in what she was doing. Then she carried on cleaning the pan she was holding. "What on earth do you mean?"

"Take me with you."

I felt my confidence beginning to crumble.

In myself.

In what I thought I *knew*.

In her.

She put the clean pan down on the drainer, turned around, dried her hands on a sodden tea towel.

My chin started to tremble.

"When you leave. With Nuncle. Take me with you."

She strode across the kitchen and wrapped me up in her

arms while my shoulders shook and my face melted into tears. She walked me over to the kitchen table, took a seat and, for the first time in a long time, hauled me up onto her lap. I hid my face on her shoulder and shook and shook and shook.

"Oh my God. Oh my poor darling," she whispered. "Don't ever think that. Not even for a second." She lifted my reluctant head from her shoulder, fixed her eyes on my weeping ones, wiped the tears from my cheeks with her thumbs. "There is nowhere in this world I'm going without you. Ever. Do you understand?" When I gave no response she gave me a little shake. "Alice, do you understand?"

I nodded. Weakly.

She let me put my head back onto her shoulder and gently rocked me.

It was true then.

Maggie came back in. "I got half a dozen pears that don't look too bad," she said. Then, seeing us, "Everything okay?"

"Alice got a bit upset, didn't you, honey? About Argyll and everything."

I looked around at Maggie and nodded. She came over and gave me a hug.

"Oh, Alice, I'm sorry," she said.

So it was true. And, from the sound of things, Maggie wouldn't be coming with us.

16

I have no idea what conversations Mum and Nuncle had in advance of this. I have no idea when and how Mum let him know that I knew and that I would be coming too. We never got a chance to talk about it.

And I don't suppose it's important anymore.

All I know is that Nuncle looked at me with a new intensity. The playfulness of the last few months was replaced with a steely seriousness.

I never discussed the plan with him, preferring to ask Mum instead. Quietly. Only when we were alone.

"When?" I would say.

"Not yet," she would answer.

Teenage girls aren't known for their patience. I only hope that I didn't pester her too badly.

(No way to ask her now, is there.)

And anyway, the agonising wait, which felt like forever to me, was really only a few weeks. While they waited for winter to exhaust itself completely, for ice to melt and snows to clear. Waiting for the moment that would give us the ghost of a chance – which was all we had – of getting out of there. And of surviving in the wild afterwards.

"When?" I asked after breakfast one morning when the rest of the family was out of the way.

"Tonight," she answered.

My heart skipped and my stomach lurched.

It wasn't exciting any more.

Instead it felt too real.

Too final.

"You don't have to do anything. I'll pack the things you need. Just be ready to leave. Okay?"

"Okay," I answered. My tongue felt thick in my mouth. My throat dry. I managed to say one thing more, "Vi?"

Mum frowned, the lines much deeper these days, while she considered this. Then she nodded. "I'll see what I can do," she said.

Which was fine. As long as Mum understood that, like she wouldn't leave without me, I wasn't going anywhere without her.

The rest of the day passed in a blur. It was as if I was outside my own body, listening without hearing, talking without knowing what I was saying. I went through the motions until bedtime when I hugged Maggie extra hard and kissed her goodnight. Then I pretended to sleep until her snoring kicked in and I could be sure she was out of it.

I lay on one side, protecting my sore shoulder, staring one last time at the coloured smears that the characters on my Snow White wallpaper had been reduced to.

For all the traumas, the deaths, the disease and hunger, for all that it had not exactly been a happy place, the farm was still the only home I had ever really known.

And I was about to leave it.

Forever.

To leave behind half of the people that I loved to be with the other half.

What sort of a decision is that to force on a fourteen year old?

I didn't then, and I still don't, consider Mum and Nuncle responsible for making me choose. Fate forced this decision on me. And where my heart led, I followed.

There was never any chance of me falling asleep accidentally and missing the signal. My heart was racing too fast and my mind along with it. So when the creak came in the corridor I immediately swung my legs over the side of the bed and inched across the room.

Not a twitch from Maggie. I stopped and drunk in the sight of her.

Goodbye, my lovely. I bent and, gentle as a breeze, kissed her cheek.

I reached for the doorknob but it started to turn by itself. For a second I was utterly confused by this but quickly realised that someone on the other side was turning it for me. I took a step back as the door swung open and there was Mum.

She put a finger to her lips.

I nodded.

She gestured for me to follow her. I did and, with infinite care, shut the door behind me. We tiptoed along the corridor, silently down the stairs, not so much as a whisper from either of us. Through the kitchen. The back door was already standing open. Mum took down my big coat from the peg by the door and I worked my way into it. I was still in my nightclothes but this would keep the cold air off me. She crouched down and got my boots. Each one had a thick sock buried in it, which she pulled out and pushed on over my feet before I wriggled them in. She quickly tied them and then stood, took down her own coat, pulled on her own boots and, wordlessly, we tiptoed out of the door. She didn't close it behind us.

The ground was soft and we made silent progress over it. I followed her around the farmhouse, up towards the sheds. This was the first surprise, I suppose. The first time that I wanted to ask her something. I'd assumed we'd be heading down over the field to the stream or maybe the taking the path to the village. So where were we going?

The big shed door was open. She led me up and inside. Nuncle was there, looking under the bonnet of the camper van. He saw us and slowly, quietly, lowered it, then pressed it closed. It made a small 'click' and we all twitched involuntarily. Mum led me to the open side door and helped me climb in. Inside there were bags and blankets and, best of all, Vi. She whimpered quietly and I knelt to greet her. *Don't worry, girl. I hadn't forgotten you. Wasn't going anywhere without you.* I hugged her and she slavered all over my face. *That's my girl.*

Mum had packed my rucksack and attached my knife in its sheath to one of the straps. She'd also laid out a change of clothes for me that I quickly swapped into for my pyjamas. She thought of everything, my mum.

The driver's side door was already open. Mum climbed into the seat and took the wheel. Nuncle was on the passenger side and started to push. The handbrake was off and the camper started to move forward. Slowly at first but then with gathering speed. Nuncle's walk turned into a gentle trot while Mum steered the van along the path at the top of the farm and towards the gap in the wall where the gate once stood.

Just like that, we were through it.

The farm was behind us.

No shouts, no alarms, no one following us.

I expected Nuncle to jump in alongside Mum so that she could start the engine but, still, he pushed. On either side of us there was only bushes where we'd cut back the trees over the years. The rutted dirt track lead to the small back lane that I'd not been driven down since I was six years old. The old camper banged and rattled over some ruts and Nuncle had to hang onto the passenger side door. Then he clambered in and shut the door behind him.

The van was trundling along quite quickly. Mum looked at him, he nodded and she turned the key. The engine turned over… and started. A low, satisfying, growl. We went along in first gear until we reached the turn for the lane. A sudden sharp left and we were on it, trundling along the pitted tarmac. Mum and Nuncle exchanged a look.

Nuncle smiled.

Mum's eyes sparkled.

And I exhaled.

"You okay, hon?" she asked, looking at me in the rear-view mirror.

I nodded. "I'm okay."

At least, I thought I was.

Nuncle half turned in his seat to look at me. "You can close the door now, munchkin." I reached across to slide the side door shut. It took a bit of effort so he leant over the back of the passenger seat to help me. The door clicked into place.

Outside the camper there was darkness all around us. "Shall I risk the headlights?" asked Mum.

"Not yet," said Nuncle. "Let's wait until we reach the road. Stay in first."

Tall hedgerows loomed up on either side of us so that it was like driving in a long, dark tunnel. Mum peered into the blackness ahead of her, gripping the wheel with grim determination. We weren't going very quickly, which helped to keep the engine noise down and gave us a fighting chance to stop in time if there was anything in the road blocking our way.

Then the hedgerows gave way as we came to a crossroads. Mum eased on the brake and we sat at the junction, engine quietly turning over, as the first stretch of real tarmacked road lay in front of us. A right turn would take us into the village. A left and we were going south to places I had no idea about.

"Left it is," said Mum.

We were on our way.

17

"Where are we going?"

It was the first time I'd felt confident enough to speak.

Nuncle and Mum smiled at one another.

"That's what I love about you, Alice. Always thinking ahead," said Mum.

"I didn't think that would be your first question," Nuncle said. "I thought you'd want to know how I got the van back up and running. With a lot or hard work and sneaking around, that's how. It's a bloody miracle, quite frankly, that it's got us this far."

"Stop admiring your own handiwork," said Mum. "Answer Alice's question."

"Quite right. We're going west," said Nuncle. "As far as the petrol will take us. Which should be far enough to put a bit of distance between us and the farm. Then we'll be on foot, I'm afraid."

"I'm not," I said. And it was true. I wasn't.

"I bet you're not," said Mum.

"Why? Are we going west, I mean?"

"The islands," said Mum. "Nuncle says they're still safe."

"I said that I think they're safe. I hope they're safe. Some of them are meant to be. At least, that's what I heard as I came north. I ran into refugees, well organised, well equipped. Not like some of the animals I met on the way. Anyway, they were heading to the coast to catch boats to the islands. It's risky, it might be bullshit, but I think it's the best chance we have."

"We wouldn't have lasted another year on the farm, hon," said Mum.

"I know."

"And your dad would never have left. It was his little kingdom and he wasn't going to leave it. Even if we starved."

I didn't answer but I knew that this, too, was true.

"What about Tom and Rich?" I asked. "And Maggie?" I felt myself getting teary.

Mum's voice was less certain now. "I know that you'll miss them, darling, so will I. But the boys aren't boys anymore. They're eighteen, grown men. They can look after themselves. And I couldn't have told them. Tom would have gone running straight to your dad, Rich would have been torn in two. It's the hardest thing I've ever had to do, much, much harder than leaving St Albans. But it's your dad that I'm leaving, not them. I just couldn't stand it any longer, hon. Oh, I could stand being cold and being hungry and being dirty and exhausted. That's something the whole world is getting used to. But I couldn't stand sharing that with someone who was even colder. You can have nothing and still make a warm, loving home, you know? You can struggle together to feed your family and keep them safe. Millions of people are doing that right now. And love is what makes it bearable, it's the only thing that makes carrying on bearable when the whole world's collapsing around you. But there was no love left in him. Not for me."

Nuncle reached over and put a hand on her arm. She'd been watching me in the rear-view mirror but turned now so she could talk to me properly. "I would never have left without you, darling. Never. So when you came to me, that was the moment. The green light. My only job now is keeping you alive, getting us somewhere we have a better chance of surviving than we did on the farm. To make a better life together."

The van lurched and she whipped her head around to correct it. "Sorry, hon, let's talk later. I need to concentrate on driving. I've not done it for a while."

"Shall we risk the headlights?" said Nuncle.

"I don't know. What do you think?"

"Either everyone for miles sees us or we drive off the road into a ditch?"

"What you're saying, Nick," she answered, "is that you'd rather risk being butchered by bandits than by my driving?"

When was the last time I heard Mum talk like this? Being herself? Sounding happy? For all that I would miss the rest of them, how could I blame Mum for wanting to be with someone who made her happy?

(Or am I being silly? Is happiness a selfish luxury when every day's a battle for survival?)

But it was nice for me to see Mum happy, if only for a few minutes. Nice for me to see her with someone who she loved and who loved her back.

It makes what happened next a bit easier to bear.

But only a bit.

18

A series of thuds.

Like rocks hitting us.

But coming from underneath the van.

The conversation about headlights was cut short as we screeched and groaned along the road. The van was all over the place, Mum fighting with the steering wheel. In the back I was thrown from one side to the other. Through the side window there was only blackness and spinning.

"Brake! Brake!" yelled Nuncle. He leant across to help Mum and held the wheel with her. "It's the tyres. They've blown out the tyres."

The van came to a stuttering, grinding stop. The over-revving engine shrieked and died. I was thrown forwards, off the seat, into the aisle between them. My head got a hefty whack as it hit the floor. Vi was scrambling, whimpering. But she recovered before I did and came to sniff at me, licking my face.

"It's okay, girl, I'm okay."

I struggled onto my feet. We were half in and half out of a ditch so that the floor was sloping to the right. I stood uneasily and rubbed the side of my head. It was sore but there was no blood.

In front of me, Mum and Nuncle were sorting themselves out. Mum's head had taken a whack on the side window and she was trying to right herself. He was hauling himself back into his seat. They clicked open their seatbelts. Mum's side of the van was up in the air so Nuncle opened the passenger-side door. It only opened a few inches before it hit dirt, so he started to kick it wide enough to wiggle out through.

Nuncle was still pushing at the door when the first figures appeared on the other side of the glass.

Two... three... four.

Then more.

Scarves tied around their faces, and not to keep out the cold. Looming out of the darkness.

Of course, I'd seen an ambush before, you already know that.

But I'd not seen one from the inside.

I'd not been the one trapped in the tin can while the mob gathered outside.

But I'd seen one. So I knew how they started.

And I knew how they ended.

If we needed to make a run for it, I wanted to be ready. I slipped my rucksack onto my back. Mum had pre-packed it for me, so I knew it would have all the essentials I needed for a foot trek through the wild to sanctuary. It had a good weight to it and felt neat and snug on my back.

Nuncle leapt back into his seat, slammed the half-open door shut behind him. He pressed the lock down and, leaning across Mum, did the same on the driver's side.

Others appeared. Some carried lit torches, adding to the terror. The flames leapt and danced, the scene an everchanging sea of light and dark. The mob began rocking the camper from either side, left and right, shaking us around like dried peas.

Nuncle reached under his seat and drew out his rifle. Not that a sniper rifle is much use in close-quarter combat.

Mum was panicked. "Don't be frightened, honey," she said. But she looked more frightened than I felt and that made it worse, not better.

Hands were grabbing at door handles, rattling them savagely. Relentlessly. Then sticks and rocks began raining onto the windscreen. It splintered and started to buckle. Nuncle levelled his rifle and shot out through it into the darkness. Trapped in our small tin can the noise was deafening. Mum screamed, fingers in her ears. Vi barked and barked and barked. But the rain of stones continued without pause.

I crouched in the aisle between the seats, one arm around Vi, another reaching around behind me for my knife. I freed it from its sheath without looking and immediately felt stronger for holding the bone handle.

The windscreen collapsed inwards. Shattered but as one piece. Hands reached in after it, clawing at Nuncle and Mum. Nuncle beat at them with the rifle stock. Another hand grabbed the barrel and Nuncle managed to let off another shot. A plume of blood, a cry of pain. Then more hands. Mum slapped them away as they groped at her. The doors were forced open and they were both dragged outside.

They disappeared into the darkness.

And the mob followed with them.

Perhaps they hadn't seen me, crouched in the back? Perhaps they didn't know that I was there?

I clambered over and into the passenger seat. My only thought was to raise the alarm. To call for help. We'd been slow and had taken the long way around on the road so we couldn't be far from the farm. Or the village. And it's not like there's any noise at night nowadays. Any unexpected sound would bring people running to help. Wouldn't it? I hit the centre of the steering wheel expecting the honk of a car horn.

Nothing.

I hit it again.

Still nothing.

They key was in the ignition and I turned it. The electrics came back on, the engine whined, I hit the horn again and this time…

Honk!

Honk!

Honk!

I pushed with both of hands, put all of my weight on it. A constant, screeching cry for help. Surely someone would hear that?

It was bound to wake the village.

Bound to wake the farm.

Help would come. It was only a matter of time.

A stocky masked figure appeared in the open door. I spun and raised my knife at him. The van's horn stopped screaming. The man reached in, grabbed at my knife arm, wrapped his bear-like arms around me and lifted me out of the van. I kicked and thrashed, kneed and butted. My knee caught him in the groin and he went down holding himself.

"Jesus Christ, Alice," he said.

I barely noticed. I ran into the dark in the direction they'd dragged Mum and Nuncle. Vi came scrambling after me.

On the road up ahead, a circle of lit torches, a crowd of masked faces.

The mob in a semi-circle with their backs to me and I dove through the middle of it, shoving and shouldering them aside, frantic to find Mum and Nuncle.

Nuncle was kneeling in the road in front of them, hands on the back of his head, fingers woven together. A masked man stood over him with a shotgun. Another carried a torch and held Mum in a tight grip at the top of one arm. Her face was cut and she was crying. A third man knelt down in front of

Nuncle so that their faces were level and removed his scarf. With his back to me I couldn't see the man's face so I moved for a better view.

My stomach lurched.

"Dad?"

He turned and looked at me. Eyes like a shark. Dead as stone.

"I'll deal with you later," he said.

I made a move towards him but strong arms held me back. I struggled against them but they held me even tighter. I turned my head and saw that it was Tom. He'd taken off his scarf and grimaced as I wrestled with him. "For God's sake, Alice, just stay still. You're in enough trouble already."

Rich came hobbling up, pained expression on his unmasked face. It was him who'd grabbed me back in the van, who I'd kicked in the balls to escape from.

"You were meant to keep her in the camper," said Tom.

"She's... she's got a kick on her," replied Rich.

"She's a fourteen-year-old girl," said Tom, clearly disgusted. He'd already forgotten how I nearly clawed his face off after Argyll died.

But I was too busy to care about their 'little sister' bullshit. My heart was racing. No, it was pounding. Heavy, brutal beats that echoed in my ears. Something dreadful was going to happen. I could feel it.

"Hello, little brother," said Dad, his face inches from Nuncle's.

"Hello, Adam. Or whatever it is you call yourself up here."

"Where do you think you're going with my wife, my daughter?" Ice-cold fury in his voice.

"Far away from here."

"In that old van? That was the best plan you could come up with? All your years as a *soldier*," he said, voice dripping with contempt, "and your getaway plan was a clapped-out old camper van? No wonder the war didn't get won."

Snickers from the mob. I thought I recognised some of them now, from their height, from their eyes. A few had removed their scarves – no more need to hide.

Villagers.

People I'd grown up with.

Gone to church with.

People my mum had fed at Christmas.

Dad had got them all out and on his side.

"Why couldn't you just let us go?" asked Nuncle. "You don't love her anymore."

"She's my wife. *My wife!*" he yelled. "What's love got to do with it?"

"Adam, what's wrong with you?" asked Mum. "You don't own me. I can go where I like."

Dad stood and walked towards her.

"And leave your family behind? Your sons? Our farm? To head off into the wilderness with this prick? The countryside's crawling with crazy people who'd kill you soon as look at you. And you'd rather risk that than look after your kids? What kind of mother are you?"

"What kind of father are you?" she said, clearly shaken. "Cold. Hateful. What sort of example are you for our sons?"

Dad lost it, raised a hand to hit her. I'd never seen him do that, not in all the years on the farm. That didn't mean he hadn't been doing it when I couldn't see. She looked back at him defiantly, daring him to strike her in front of so many witnesses. His face was a mask of hate, jaw clenched, muscles grinding away under the skin. But he stopped, regathered himself, lowered his arm. Turned his attention back to Nuncle.

"Is that why you came back? To sneak away with her, first chance you got?"

"No. I was looking for a home. Like everyone else. The farm was the last one I had. When I set off north I wasn't even sure you'd still be there. Then I saw how you treated her, how unhappy she was. And I wanted to get her away..."

"How romantic," said Dad. He was playing to his audience now. "But you're not as clever as you think. And we're not as stupid. You think all that sneaking around wasn't noticed? Your little scouting expeditions, scrounging for parts, oil, petrol?" (Well I hadn't noticed a thing, so Nuncle was clearly cleverer than me.) "The local militia's been watching you for months. And Tom, Rich. So when you made a run for it, we were all ready for you." He spoke like this was a revelation, a masterstroke. I expected Nuncle to be surprised.

Instead, he laughed.

And laughed and laughed and laughed.

Which I don't think Dad was expecting, either.

"Militia?" he said. Now it was Nuncle's voice dripping with sarcasm. "Oh my God, you and your militia games. Do you know how ridiculous you sound? Playing soldiers up here, a thousand miles away from the fighting? The militias don't exist anymore. They packed up years ago. Half the country's under military rule. Not that things are any better. You either fall in with the regular army or you're executed. That's it. That's how it works. It will take them a while to get up here, but they will. They're very, very thorough." The mob was silent, suddenly unsure of itself. "By the way, where's your pal, *Captain* Smith? Past his bedtime is it?"

"No but Smith and I have already spoken on this matter. From what you've already told us, Nick, you are a deserter. And in time of war there is only one punishment for deserters. Execution."

Nuncle almost looked amused.

"Are you serious?"

But Mum was nervous, I could hear it in her voice. She knew Dad better. Knew that he was always serious. "Don't be ridiculous, Adam. What right do you have?"

"The right of a husband. The right of a father," he yelled back at her. "By rights we should march him to the nearest military outpost. But there isn't one. And why the Hell should we risk the lives of our own people, out in the wild? In which case sentence will be carried out summarily. Right here. Right now."

Dad nodded to a couple of the mob. They hauled Nuncle to his feet, dragged him backwards, stood him up against the chest-high stone wall that ran either side of the road. Nuncle was almost too baffled to react.

"Adam, no! Stop this now. Stop this and I'll come home. It will be just the same as it was. I'm begging you, Adam. Stop this," Mum pleaded.

It was my turn to scream. "No, Dad, no!" I could taste sick in the back of my throat, felt my knees start to buckle.

It must have dawned on Nuncle that Dad was serious and he began to resist, kicking and thrashing his legs around, sending up a scree of dirt and pebbles. More of the mob joined the men at the wall, pushed Nuncle back against the stone, pinioned his arms out to the sides. Like a scarecrow. "Adam, you're out of your mind," he shouted. "I'm you brother. Who's gonna do it? You? One of these wankers?"

Dad signalled to a torch-bearer who stepped forward from his position in the semi-circle. "No, he is. Militia Commander Stevens. You shot his son Barry in the face ten minutes ago. He bled to death by the roadside."

Dad handed Nuncle's rifle to Stevens and took the torch off him. Stevens pulled aside the scarf. His face was smeared with tears and blood. (Not, I immediately understood, his own.) I recognised him. He'd come up to the farm with Smith a few times. I'd seen him chatting happily with Argyll. We'd fed him at Christmas.

"One shot," said Dad as Stevens positioned himself in the middle of the road.

Mum was babbling now. "Adam? Adam? Don't do this. Let him go, please let him go. I'll do anything. We can move back in together. Try for another child. Anything. Anything."

Stevens raised the rifle to his shoulder.

Levelled it.

Checked the sight.

A sniper rifle to kill a man twelve feet away? I could make that shot. He wouldn't miss. It wasn't possible.

Then Mum lashes out. Has broken free of the hand gripping her.

She is running towards Nuncle. Covering the space between her and him in a heartbeat.

Her last.

(Moments I relive in my head every time I close my eyes.)

The rifle cracks.

A single shout.

Mum is hanging from Nuncle's shoulders. Blood is pooling through her clothes. Her legs can't support her. Her weight is pulling them both down.

I think I was screaming. But it was like I wasn't inside my own body anymore. Tom lets go and I run towards her, wrap my arms around her shoulders as she slumps to her knees.

Nuncle's knees have buckled, too. From her weight and his own. High-calibre, army-issue sniper rifles can pierce body armour a mile away. The bullet that ripped into my mum's back carried right on, out of her chest and into Nuncle's. Then out through his spine before splintering against the wall.

Blood is pouring from the hole in his chest. His arms are limp, hers clutch his shoulders. Their last seconds are spent seeing only each other. I clutch at Mum's hair, rub my face against hers. I have no idea if I am saying anything.

But her last words, as the light left her eyes and all the light left my world. Little more than a whisper in Nuncle's ear. "Look at her, Nick."

His eyes flicker towards me as he dies.

"She's yours, Nick. She's yours."

19

What happened immediately after that, I have no memory of.

20

It must have been quite easy for me to slip away in the chaos. I say 'must have' because I really don't have a clue. I suppose that I ran and lost myself in the dark. Thank goodness Vi ran with me. At some point my senses returned and I knew only where I was not.

But I remembered Nuncle saying that we were going to go west.

To the islands.

Where hope still existed.

And so, even though I had no hope, that's what I kept doing.

Going west.

The orphan girl and her dog.

(Because when your mum and dad are dead you're an orphan, right?)

Starting each day with the sun behind me and walking towards each sunset.

Running. Hiding. Scavenging.

Until fate brought me here.

To a beach at the edge of the world.

I still have lots to tell. But I'm tired and I'd like to sleep now. The driftwood fire is warm and orange sparks are dancing from it, mingling with the stars overhead. Further along the beach there are more campfires, strung like pearls on a necklace along the semi-circle of the bay. Around each fire more survivors of the wreckage, each with their own story to tell. Stories of terror, pain and loss told by the cold, the frightened and the hungry.

And the alone.

I'm so glad I'm not one of them. Alone, I mean. I hug Vi closer to me and she whimpers. Her fur and warmth are a blessing. Her teeth, too, will come in very useful if anyone decides to get too curious about the fourteen-year-old girl on the beach. I have my dagger as well and all the skills that Argyll taught me.

(Argyll, who is dead now.)

These three things have kept me alive and carried me this far. To the edge of the land. To a white sand beach beyond which, somewhere out across the black water, just a short boat ride away (so everyone tells me) lie the last sanctuaries. Island communities where hope still lives. Where order still remains. The last little boats, loaded with refugees, left before sunset as only a lunatic would try to make the crossing after dark. (The sea has already claimed its share of lunatics.) But there is tension in the air and uncertainty, mutterings in the dark.

Will the boats come again tomorrow?

If so, how many?

Enough to take us all?

What if they don't come?

What will become of us?

There's a bigger, unanswerable question that no one asks but I suspect we're all thinking. What will become of us even if the boats do return?

Some people have waited longer than others, many days and nights, and are anxious in case newcomers get ahead of them in the queue. Hundreds have already passed this way and more continue to gather. But, from what I've seen, the people wait quite patiently for their own turn to arrive. The boatsmen demand order at the water's edge and immediately threaten to leave if there's pushing and shoving, which keeps us all in check.

And so, in the morning, I will rejoin the queue that snakes around the dying fires and trudge to the edge of the sea. Like I did yesterday. And the day before. We all hope it will not rain, or be foggy, or that breakers will make it impossible for the boats to get close enough to pick us up. I was close today, closer than the day before, tomorrow I will be closer.

Tomorrow it will be my turn. I know it will.

But I'm tired now and I'd like to sleep.

Will I dream? Of the farm? Of the family I've lost?

So many bad things happened there but there was love and laughter, too.

It was the place where Mum's love surrounded me.

Where Maggie slept snoring next to me.

The place of my brothers' endless teasing and Argyll's teaching.

If I do dream, I hope it's of the good things and not the bad.

But best not to get my hopes up, eh?

I lie down, using Vi's flanks as a pillow, pull my one, thin blanket over me and look at the stars.

I wonder if, out there, billions of miles away, there's another girl doing the exact same thing right now.

Even if there is, I bet she doesn't have stag's blood in her veins.